Bound by passion. Freed by love.

When the damaged and torme...... equally broken Logan, they embark on a torrid, emotionally provocative affair that irrevocably changed their lives. Emma has sacrificed her entire being and just when she thinks Logan is willing to do the same, he holds back. Reluctant for their love to be a thing of shadows, Emma issues an ultimatum: commit or say goodbye. Fearful of losing her, Logan agrees.

In order to keep her, he must gain permission to marry from the one man he's sought to avoid: his brother, the King. His appeal is denied and instead, Logan is seized and sent to the dungeon with no hope for escape. While in Hell, Logan's dark past haunts him, threatening to consume him. He must fight to remain the man he's become with Emma by his side and relinquish the control he's held onto for a lifetime.

Fearing her lover is dead, Emma decides once and for all she must leave history where it belongs and return to the present. But when she tries once again to break the bonds of time, she is struck down. Emma must choose her destiny. Must answer the cries her body makes in the dark for her laird. They've always been strongest when together, but now Emma must find the courage on her own to see her fate fulfilled—and Logan returned to her.

Praise for *BEHIND THE PLAID*...

4 ½ stars and a Top Pick from Night Owl Romance! *"Wickedly sinful, arousingly erotic, and delightfully delicious, Logan is the stuff that naughty Highlander dreams are made of."*

DARK SIDE OF THE LAIRD

Book Three – Highland Bound Trilogy

By
Eliza Knight

****

FIRST EDITION
December 2013

Copyright 2013 © Eliza Knight

Cover Design by Kimberly Killion @ The Killion Group, Inc.

****

Also Available by Eliza Knight

Behind the Plaid (Book 1: Highland Bound)
Bared to the Laird (Book 2: Highland Bound)
The Rebound Pact – A Sexy Contemporary
A Kilted Christmas Wish – A Sexy Contemporary Novella
The Highlander's Reward – Book One, The Stolen Bride Series
The Highlander's Conquest – Book Two, The Stolen Bride Series
The Highlander's Lady – Book Three, The Stolen Bride Series
The Highlander's Warrior Bride – Book Four, The Stolen Bride Series
The Highlander's Triumph – Book Five, The Stolen Bride Series
The Highlander's Sin – Book Six, The Stolen Bride Series
A Lady's Charade (Book 1: The Rules of Chivalry)
A Knight's Victory (Book 2: The Rules of Chivalry)
A Gentleman's Kiss
Men of the Sea Series: *Her Captain Returns, Her Captain Surrenders, Her Captain Dares All*
The Highland Jewel Series: *Warrior in a Box, Lady in a Box, Love in a Box*
Lady Seductress's Ball
Take it Off, Warrior
Highland Steam
A Pirate's Bounty
Highland Tryst (Something Wicked This Way Comes Volume 1)
Highlander Brawn (Sequel to *Highland Steam*)

Coming soon…

The Highlander's Temptation (Prequel: The Stolen Bride Series)

Writing under the name E. Knight

Coming soon…

My Lady Viper – Tales From the Tudor Court
Prisoner of the Queen – Tales From the Tudor Court

Writing under the name Annabelle Weston

Wicked Woman (Desert Heat)
Scandalous Woman (Desert Heat)
Notorious Woman (Desert Heat)
Mr. Temptation
Hunting Tucker

****

Visit Eliza Knight at www.elizaknight.com or
www.historyundressed.com

DEDICATION

*For every woman who's ever dreamed of a Highlander of their own,
long may Logan bless your dreams...*

ACKNOWLEDGEMENTS

*Many thanks to my wonderful readers! I'm so blessed to have you all
and I'm so incredibly grateful that you've enjoyed these stories.*

Dark Side of the Laird

PROLOGUE

Emma

Five months earlier…

*T*his night would forever change me.

The storm raged. Stinging pelts of rain spiking against my cheekbones. Hair whipping into my eyes. I held my hands up, trying in vain to halt the rain as it blurred my vision from the castle rising in the dark, its tower ruins kissing the midnight sky.

Lightning flashed, startling me, jolting through my veins and then I was hurled to the ground. Somewhere in the distance I heard the cab driver tell me to come back. A voice that sounded disturbingly not like my own told him to go.

And then I woke, warmed by a different sun. A different time. No longer was I at the castle ruins of Gealach, but a place far altered. The castle stood tall, proud, and imposing. Each stone in its place, a shingled roof, and heavy wooden doors. Gone were the piles of rock and haunting ravens that pecked at what was left of any rotting wood.

Even still, the place was haunting, eerie in its quietness. And then the air started to vibrate. Literally pulsing around me. My skin tingled, hair on the back of my neck stood on end, vision blurred.

I could hear things that weren't there. Voices. Shouts. Metal. I could smell things that were weren't there. Animals, hay, peat fires and… fear.

And then nothing.

All at once, it caved in around me, dragging me down in an overload of senses that made me cough and choke on an empty gag.

Cries of panic. Shouts of warning.

Startling utter silence.

Then more noise… clanging, running, screaming.

I crawled up the stone stairs feeling like every inch was a feat. My fingers scraping on the stone, I dragged myself to the top, intent on getting inside and away from what was sure to be my undoing.

Fingertips on the cool iron handle, I had it. But I couldn't make it budge. Whatever the noise and the smell, they were draining me, taking away every ounce of energy I possessed.

Was this punishment for running away from my husband? For leaving a marriage that was so very unpleasant, I might have flung myself from a window if I'd not been given the number for a cab service by the woman whose inn we stayed at for our holiday?

I don't know… This felt…awful.

Fear rushed like a torrent of waves through my veins making me shake, sweat, and freezing me in a moment of terror.

The door wouldn't budge and with each passing second my heart beat faster and I couldn't quite catch my breath.

"Open," I said, but the words didn't come out. Either that or the noise inside my head drowned out my plea.

I closed my eyes, praying both that I'd wake up at the inn with my husband, Steven, standing over me, just as much as I swore I never wanted to see him again. Which was it? I knew with all my heart I didn't ever want to see Steven again. But this nightmare...

Could be a new life. This is what escape was supposed to be about. Getting away from him. Leaving him for good. Starting out on my own and learning just who I had become—a shadow of my former self. A shell with its guts ripped out. I was empty. Soulless.

I tugged on the handle again, hard, knowing this could be the start of something new. I had to move forward. This time it gave way. Gave way so hard, I went tumbling backward, elbow hitting the stone hard and landing on my hip at the bottom.

"What the—" But the words stilled on my tongue, for there, standing at the top of the stone stairs, taking up the expanse of the monstrous wooden door was the devil himself.

A Scottish warrior. Broad, muscular, dark. He was dressed in a red and green kilt and billowing shirt, tall boots and weapons covered his entire being. His dark hair was pulled back but wisps of it beat against his forehead and his murderous eyes.

His features were sharp, chiseled from stone. Darkly handsome. Wickedly sensual. Currents of longing and fear clashed inside me. I opened my mouth to speak but was too afraid of what would come out.

The people addressed him as laird. He was the lord of this place. But I could have guessed that. Power oozed from his every pore. Every taut, rippling muscle screamed of strength.

He addressed me. Came down the stairs and reached out a hand. Now was the time to make a decision. Take his hand or run. On the outside, the laird was only offering to help me up, but I knew in reality… This offer was so much more than that. The promise of it was in his eyes. The way he assessed me and the way I shivered in response. Shivers I'd never felt before. A need, a craving that was so new and penetrating it nearly stopped my heart from beating.

Little did I know when I escaped Steven that I'd be hurled headlong into the arms of a dark and dangerous Highlander. A warrior who with one look could make me burn.

The grass below me had to be singed, from not only the intensity of his stare, but the way my body heated in response.

I could hardly look back now. Instead, I warily looked forward, certain I was seeing the most dark side of this laird, and wanting desperately to sink inside his soul.

CHAPTER ONE

Emma

Scottish Highlands
Late November, 1542

"Steady that horse, or I'll have you run through!"

The king's shout from the courtyard had me rushing to the small window and flinging open a shutter to see who he spoke with.

Heart beating fast, I knew the king wouldn't shout at Logan that way, so I had no cause to fear for his safety, but there was always that lingering thought that he'd come crashing down on the brother whom he wanted no one to know about. The secret to which a kingdom could fall. What had Logan said? That he held the key to the future of Scotland and the power to tear the country apart.

I shuddered. It was enough to make me fear ever advising him against his king. Except... The king was hell bent on destroying not only Logan, but myself, it would seem.

A thin lad gripped the reins of a horse easily a foot taller than him and nearly a thousand pounds heavier. It was a beautiful chestnut with a snowy white mane, chest and forelegs. I didn't know much about horseflesh, but even I could tell it was an expensive breed.

The king clunked toward him, his armor chinking with each step. He raised his hand and whacked the poor boy on the back of his head. The sound echoed up the stones to my window. I cringed and jerked as though I'd been hit myself. The boy stifled a cry, biting his trembling lip and though I couldn't see it, I could only assume tears pooled in his eyes. In the months I'd been at Gealach I'd grown to love and respect the people.

My heart constricted for the young squire. I couldn't have been more proud of the young boy if he'd been my own, though. For he didn't cry out. Didn't glare up at the man who treated him with injustice, and with one swift word could have him killed for what he would perceive as insolence. The boy simply bowed his head and appeared to murmur apologies.

Logan's cruel brother — the people's king! — snarled.

Evident then, were the many differences between Logan and his brother. Logan was fierce and powerful, a man no one wanted to trifle with. He put fear into his enemies. But he wasn't a bully to anyone. He was a protector. He commanded respect, but he gave enough that he deserved it. King James was just an asshole.

A cocky son of a bitch that didn't deserve a second glance, wouldn't have gotten one in a modern era, but here, he commanded all.

I glowered down at him, safe in my room and away from prying eyes to see my contempt.

The man had come to the castle over a week ago and raised hell since he'd arrived. It was all Logan could do to keep his clan's sanity in check. They all abhorred the king, and I couldn't imagine how that made Logan feel—knowing his past.

He could have been—should have been—king. What a better monarch he would have made, too.

Born the first of fraternal twins to a dying queen, Logan was considered the weaker of the babes and a problem. The king had ordered him killed the night he was born, but several servants couldn't see the deed done, believing that killing an innocent child would send them straight to hell. Instead, under the cover of darkness they sent him to live with the Highland lord and lady that Logan had grown up thinking were his parents. Only on the king's deathbed did an elderly servant confess their grievous sin, and in turn that dying king relayed it to James.

I suppose Logan should feel blessed his brother didn't see him murdered straight away, for Logan was the rightful king. But that didn't make it any less wrong that he should so thoroughly have Logan clutched by the balls.

The king growled something else at the boy who scampered off, a look of relief on his face. One of King James' knights stepped forward and held the reins as he put his foot in the stirrup and then lifted himself onto the horse's back. Metal scraped on leather. He settled himself in the saddle and barked an order to a few of his men to prepare for departure.

Wait! Where was Lady Isabella?

The vicious wench should be leaving with the king. I frantically searched the crowd of riders. She'd arrived with him after all. Stoic, beautiful and utterly cruel, Lady Isabella had been brought to Gealach by the king—his intention to write a betrothal contract between her and my man. But she was a MacDonald, niece to Logan's enemy, and the one man who threatened the kingdom's safety beyond the two silently feuding brothers.

Logan had not agreed to marry her despite the king's insistence — at least that I knew of.

Oh, my God... Had he changed his mind, in favor of appeasing the king? He'd promised that he'd never choose that woman over me. That he would seek the king's permission to marry me.

A promise I'd been all too hopeful for. Deep down, I must have known it could only ever be a dream. I loved Logan with an intensity that was probably unhealthy — but that was wholly a part of me. I couldn't live without him. He was a part of my soul. Too good to be true. Was that why it was so easy to believe he might have changed his mind? Because if he wanted to live in peace with his brother he was better off marrying Lady Isabella. But I knew better. Logan would never do anything that could damage the country's safety, the people's freedom, and marrying Isabella was only bound to do just that.

I'd agreed to marry him only after lamenting that he'd be destroying the unstable relationship he had with his brother. King James was bound to be pissed that Logan was going against his wishes. The ornery man would wage war, no doubt. *That* I couldn't allow. Not for all the love in the world. And, wow, did I love the man. Fiercely. Hauntingly. Obsessively.

No matter how many times I'd tried to get back to my own time, Fate had kept me pinned to his side. We were bound. In some vision of destiny, we were meant to be together, heedless of time limits.

If Isabella weren't leaving today, I might have murdered her. I was not a violent person, but she grated on my nerves more than anyone I'd ever met — and it was more than the fact that she was trying to steal Logan. She was alluring, seductive, and tempting. A real bitch. A home-wrecker.

The king shouted a final order before turning his mount around in the courtyard and pushing him into a trot. Without a helmet, his hair flopped in the wind. He filed out the gate of Gealach in a line with his men and servants. The entire caravan marching with purpose, flags raised and trumpets blaring.

"No," I whispered, searching the rows of riders for Isabella's back. No women.

Where was Lady Isabella?

Then a flash of red caught my eye. Standing directly below my window was the tart. Dark, glossy hair perfectly coiffed. A gown as elegant and regal as a queen. She shimmered, literally. So many jewels clasped to her fingers, neck, wrists, even her gown. They sparkled in the sunlight. Isabella waved a red, silk scarf in the air at the departing caravan. The way it wafted in the breeze with such peaceful intent filled me with rage. I wanted to trample her like a bull when taunted by a matador.

She was staying. No freaking way.

I slapped the stone casement of the window. A flash of memory spiraled through my mind—Logan's heavy, erotic breathing, the feel of his hands on my naked breasts as he'd pounded into me while I leaned over this very spot. However much the thought should have heated me, I was filled with an icy dread.

Isabella was going to make my life a living, breathing hell.

As the last of the horses rode beneath the gates and the gatekeepers rushed to close the heavy wooden doors, the woman peered up at me. She'd known I was there all along. The cruel smile that peeled her lips back had me gritting my teeth. Her gray eyes, which I'd once thought were dull and lifeless, were in fact quite heavy with negative sentiment—mean and calculating. The bitch knew I wanted her to leave. Knew that I was against the king's wish for her to marry Logan.

He was mine.

And she was determined to see that she was the only one he ended up with. Lady Isabella had a plan up her sleeve and given that her uncle was the worst of Logan's enemies, I had a feeling that her plan was hatched not of her own accord but greedily accepted when broached.

I watched with mounting dread and pain in my heart as the king's caravan rode over the dirt-packed road, disappearing over the ridge and rising again until all that was left of them was a cloud of dirt.

No one had returned for Isabella. No one in the courtyard seemed confused by her presence. I wanted to scream in frustration to shred the shutters from the stone and toss them down on her head.

I could do none of those things. To the outside world, and even to Isabella, I was nothing. She'd asked me and I'd told her that there was nothing between Logan and I. Having woman's intuition, she'd guessed that he and I were an item. How could she not? The way we stared at each other across a room was hot enough to light a fire in the hearth.

I was screwed.

If Logan had indeed told King James that he wouldn't marry Isabella, then the only reason she was here was because the king had chosen for her to remain behind in hopes of changing Logan's mind. Maybe she wanted to seduce him. If he got her pregnant he'd be bound to her. Wasn't that the way of things in this era? Even though I trusted Logan not to go after her… Isabella was a conniving, deceitful woman.

Despite her nature, Lady Isabella *was* a noblewoman and *the* bride the king had chosen for Logan. Just as I'd suspected, there was little he could do to get out of it. He was bound, more so than anyone else, to his brother and what the king chose for him as his fate.

Damn it. I slammed the shutters closed and stomped my foot, feeling powerless. I wouldn't let Isabella come between us, and I just couldn't share.

The thought of it made me physically ill. I doubled over, clutching at my belly.

Going back to my own time was out of the question. I felt too deeply for Logan to go back to that life. And I was scared of what I'd find there. My husband—*ex* was what I considered him—was a vicious worm. I shook my head. No way was I ever going back to him. Steven was dead to me. Logan was my future.

Another inaudible shout had me opening the shutters again, in desperate hopes that the king had realized Isabella was left behind. But all that greeted me was the normal routines of the castle's inhabitants. How awful that everything should appear so normal when I felt so off.

Outside the trees were nearly barren, a few straggling red and orange leaves hanging on to branches as though their lives depended on it. They refused to let go, clinging to the tree with every last ounce of strength they had.

Much like me clinging to Logan and this time, fearful of the time when nature took its course and I would have no choice but to let go, swirling down into the depths of some place I didn't want to be. Dying.

I turned from the window and trudged over to the chair. My cold breakfast looked pathetic in its austerity. I sat down determined to eat the bowl of porridge which had long since formed into a hardened blob of mush. Tunnels of honey and almond milk made rivulets in the center of the oats.

I'd barely slept in the last week since Logan had taken me through the secret door. The one I'd been through on my own before. The one that scared the shit of me. Down a hundred stairs and into the hidden chamber, he'd led me. Shown me the maps on the doors. Doors that represented different fates—life, death, honor and the unknown. Logan had opened up to me. Trusted me and shared with me the secrets of the castle. The thing that startled me the most was unearthing yet another clue that proved I was meant to be here. Evidenced by the rune tattoo on my hip was the same as the one etched onto the door holding a sealed treasure box, the contents of which even Logan wasn't privy to. He trusted me. And I trusted him. That was all that should matter.

"Emma."

I glanced up, startled.

From the doorway, Logan cleared his throat, his face serious, worry lines etched at the corners of his dark eyes. His black hair was pulled back in a queue, longer than it was when I'd arrived at his stone fortress some months before. His shoulders were broad, nearly as wide as the door frame, and he had to duck an inch to get inside. Long, muscular legs. Thick, sculpted arms. Chiseled chest and abs. All regretfully covered except for his athletic calves. He stared at me intently, as though he would know everything that went on inside my head, my heart. Like he wanted to devour my soul, and lord help me, I would hand it to him on a silver platter.

I tossed my linen napkin onto the table and started to stand.

He held up his hand, staying me. "Nay, dinna get up. Your meal will get cold."

"Too late," I said with a nervous laugh staring at the stiffened porridge that appeared to have taken on a gray hue.

He stalked toward me, the way he always did. Sensual, powerful and determined. My body immediately came alive, recalling how many delicious things often happened in the wake of his pursuing me. Hot, torrid, dangerous.

His thighs brushed my forearm as he stopped right beside my chair and I craned my neck to look up at him, taking in his raw, dangerous beauty. Logan leaned down, his eyelids lowering and I swallowed as his lips neared mine.

Every kiss made me shiver. Every kiss excited me. Every kiss made me want to strip bare. This one was no different. I sank back in my chair, unable to hold myself steady, and he followed me, lips on fire. Logan tantalized me with his tongue, skating it over my lips, sinking it into my mouth only to withdraw when I touched mine to his. He teased me, taunted me, until I was breathless and then he pulled away, a satisfied smile on his lips.

He knew what his kisses did to me, how they made me feel and he liked it. Cherished it. Aspired to it. I was a hot and bothered mess. Goosebumps up and down my arms. Nipples hard as stones, slick sex, clenching thighs, breath heaving.

"Ye've not eaten or slept in days," he murmured.

I nodded, watching the way his body unfolded in the chair opposite mine, legs stretched out, his bare knees poking from beneath his pleated plaid.

"Tell me," he urged, steepling his fingers beneath his chin and studying me.

"What?" I shrugged. "There is nothing to tell."

"Tell me what is on your mind."

I chewed on my lip. He'd promised me that he'd speak to the king. Promised me that we'd be together. And yet… "Lady Isabella is still here."

Logan's eyes narrowed and lips turned down in a frown. "Aye."

He didn't elaborate. Just *aye*. What the hell was I supposed to say to that? Frustration mounted inside me and old insecure monsters reared their heads. I shoved them down, beat them down. Logan had never made me feel small, insignificant. He'd never told me I was worthless. Never made me feel like less of a person than Steven did. If anything, he'd worshipped me.

I waited, holding my breath. When a number of moments ticked by and my lungs started to burn I let it out, sat forward, my eyes locked on his.

"Aye?"

He nodded. "Not of my choosing."

"Did you…speak to the king at all about us?"

Again he nodded, but slowly. "Aye."

My breath hitched. "Logan —"

Sensing my frustration he cut me off. "My desires were not met well by my liege."

I nodded having deciphered that much on my own.

"I kept your name hidden from him, though I'm guessing he surmised that 'twas ye." Logan pushed out of the chair and walked to the window, pulling back my shutters and looking out. He crossed his arms over his chest, tense all over.

I approached him, slipping my arms around his waist from behind, leaning my cheek against his back.

"He can't win," I said.

"I fear he already has."

CHAPTER TWO

Logan

*'T*was hard to keep my anger in check when every inch of me felt the intense urge to leap upon my horse and chase the king down. At every turn, James had been there making decisions without regard for me. Over the last dozen years, he'd bribed me with gifts—bawdy women, barrels of fine wine, jewels, silver. And I'd been happy to tilt my head in thanks and receive my gifts with pleasure. But lately, his enticements had not...enticed me. Not with Emma showing me what I'd been missing.

Since she'd walked into my life, I'd never been the same. And I'd realized something—that those gifts had been a means of shutting me up. Of making me bend to his will. Of doing his dirty work. I'd been ruled round for over a dozen years by that spoiled piece of shite.

I gritted my teeth, keeping my anger on a tight leash so as not to scare Emma. The lass had been through enough — more than enough. Hell, she wasn't even from this time. Five hundred years separated her from now and where she came from. I couldn't say belonged, because I felt she belonged here with me. Her time-travel didn't bother me at all. Magic happened frequently when the stars aligned and it wasn't something I'd been foreign to. There were others who proclaimed to have come from another place. Though her travel was a fact I'd only just learned recently, 'haps in my heart I had known all along.

I'd been drawn to her like a ship to a beacon light upon the land, she led me home, centered me.

Her coming here had been a blessing for me, though I wasn't entirely sure it was a blessing for her, even if the signs pointed to it being both our destinies.

"We will need to give him more time, 'tis all," I managed to say, though even I could hear the strangle in my voice.

Emma stared up at me skeptically.

"Time?" She hooked her thumb toward the window. "I don't think all the time in the world is going to help now. He's left Isabella here. With you. What will you do about her?"

Any thought of Isabella left a sour taste in my mouth. I'd just as soon toss her onto a hole-riddled ship and have her guide herself home. Fate would either lead her to safety or the choppy waters of the sea would swallow her and her evil intentions. "Ignore her the best I can."

"And what if she…" I watched the play of emotions across Emma's face. Lord, she was being tormented by her vivid imaginings of illicit happenings.

I leaned forward, eyes locking on hers, gripped her shoulders and gave her a reassuring squeeze. "I will not allow her to come near me. Dinna fear for me, or her. I swear to ye, Emma, she will not come between us."

Emma nodded, chewing one of her luscious lips. She gripped onto my shirt and tugged me closer, gazing up at me as though she'd memorize my face. "I don't want to spend our time together worrying." She glanced away a moment before looking back. "I never know how much time we'll have."

A reminder that her time here was not guaranteed. Even if she'd tried unsuccessfully twice now to get back to her own era, did not mean the tides of time couldn't change their minds.

"Let us not worry then. Let us simply enjoy each other's company." I skimmed my lips over hers, feeling her sink against me, relaxing somewhat into my embrace. I massaged the tense muscles of her back and deepened the kiss, slanting my lips harder over hers, my tongue darting in and out of her mouth, teasing, tasting.

Whenever I touched her, the world, my troubles, haunting demons, all vanished and it was just the two of us, her healing touch captivating me, pulling me in, drowning me in everything that was her.

I growled in the back of my throat, body suddenly on fire with need for her. Cock hard, muscles tense, I lifted her up and carried her over to the bed. With each encounter, I tried to teach her a lesson in lovemaking, tried to bring her to new heightened levels of sensitivity and restraint, but not this time.

Nay, right now I just needed her. Needed to feel her warmth all around me, needed to drown inside her instead of thinking about what James had said to me earlier that morning. Needed to forget the wench who would do her damnedest to put herself between Emma and I.

"I need ye," I said to her, tossing her onto the bed and covering her with my body, feeling every lush curve against my hardness.

"Yes, take me."

I shoved her gown up swiftly around her hips, slid my hands up her thigh and dipped my fingers against the wet dew of her folds.

"Och, ye're already so wet," I said, kissing her hard, owning her with the simple prod of my tongue as I thrust two fingers inside her tight, wet, hot sheath.

"Always," she murmured against my mouth, moaning and bucking her hips upward. She spread her thighs wide, nails raking down the linen back of my shirt.

I hiked up my plaid, taking hold of my stiff cock and notching the head to her opening.

"I canna wait," I said, needing to pound inside her.

"Don't."

All the permission I needed. I let intensity take hold. I thrust inside her, arching my hips upward just as she tilted hers. A perfect fit. Deep inside her clenching quim, I started to feel whole. Every exquisite inch withdrew in tumultuous rushes of sensation. I thrust back in, deeper, hitting the knot of flesh at the top of her sheath and listening to her hiss in pleasure and pain.

What a pair we were.

"Faster," she said, her body clenching, the wet walls of her cunny gripping me tight. Already, she was close to climaxing.

I pumped faster, our hips clashing together in tune to the sounds of the bed scraping on the floorboards. I took her hands in mine, threading our fingers and bringing them up over her head as I pushed and pulled my hips to hers.

Emma brought her legs up higher, gripping them tight to my waist as she used her abdominal muscles to lift her buttocks from the bed and hold them there, letting me go deeper, letting each pound of my pelvis to hers slam against that tiny bundle of nerves—her clit as she'd named it.

Every thrust, every pull, she moaned and gasped. I loved her response. Loved everything about her. Loved that she healed me with her touch and made me want to be a better man.

I captured her lips again in a searing kiss, feeling her tighten all the more. She was close. My cock lurched with sudden a sudden furious need, feeling that hot and cold sensation burn its way up and down my length. Then climax gripped me. Still I held it at bay, trying desperately to maintain some control, but then she bucked, cried out against my lips and I was lost. Control forgotten, relinquished in exchange for a leap into ecstasy. She cried out, her entire form quaking violently. Her wet channel sucking me in further as it fluttered with release.

"Oh, Emma," I growled, biting her lower lip a little harder then I should.

She whimpered, then bit me back.

I chuckled, slowing my pace until a few lazy thrusts were all I could manage, then rolled to the side and pulled her into my arms.

"Thank ye," I murmured.

"For what?"

"For taking my mind off the sniveling tart for a few moments."

Emma laughed, though I could tell that beneath her bluster, she was pained by Isabella's presence.

"I will try my damnedest to send her away," I said.

"Can you do that?"

"The deed will not please my brother. In fact, he will undoubtedly punish me for it, but it can be done. She likely will not leave willingly, so I'd have to truss her up and have her escorted by my men."

"Does she reside near her uncle?"

"Wouldn't be surprised if she lived with that bastard."

"Just don't send her back the way you sent him."

I couldn't help a laugh. That MacDonald swine had tried on so many occasions to harm my clan, to kill me. The last time he came, he even threatened the life of the king. Proclaiming himself Lord of the Isles and future king of Scotland.

I'd sent him back to his northern isles shackled to his ship with the very manacles he'd brought in chests to enslave my people. When he'd returned yet again, I'd shown him my idea of hospitality in the dungeons, but he'd escaped, and now his niece roamed freely within my castle.

"She is his spy," I said, wondering what the wench was up to at that moment.

Emma nodded, her head bouncing against my shoulder. "Looking for your secrets right now even."

"Under MacDonald's instruction."

"That, and because she wants to trap you."

"Trap me?"

"Into marriage."

"Hmm. I dinna know whether she truly wants to marry me."

Emma snorted. "Please, Logan, she was practically growling and peeing on your leg as though that might ward off any other women."

"I'm glad she didna do that."

"Me, too. What a mess that would have been."

"Aye." I stood and pulled her up, too. "I've got to meet with Ewan. What have you planned for your day?"

She smoothed out her gown and frowned. "Nothing quite yet. With Isabella lurking around, I might just stay in my chamber."

"Dinna let her get to ye." Anger at the wretched intruder made me scowl. Emma didn't deserve to be a slave to her chamber.

"What choice do I have? I don't want to have her confront me."

"'Haps she'll ignore ye. Ye made it clear we had no designs on each other."

Emma pursed her lips. "Yes. But woman's intuition is…"

"Usually right."

28

"Just as I said, someone may be coercing Isabella to marry you—the king and her brother—but that doesn't mean she doesn't want to." She wrapped her arms around my neck. "You are one handsome, charismatic, intense man. I've wanted you from the moment I met you."

"So ye think she desires me?" I wiggled my brows and tucked my arms around her waist so she couldn't escape me.

"You're a brute." Emma pouted in a way that made me want to take her to bed again. To prove how much a brute I was not, and how much she was the only woman for me.

"I'm sure Cook would love your help in the gardens, picking last minute harvests. Maybe even helping with storing everything for winter. With the first frost already coming, the crops are in danger of being ruined."

Emma sighed. "You've convinced me. You know, I never knew how much I liked gardening and watching food grow before I came here."

I chuckled. "And how did you grow your food before?"

She gave me a worried look. "You're going to think this is odd, but I bought it at a market. We had these great big buildings filled with food, all year round. It was shipped from warmer places in winter or greenhouses, fresh things in crates and non-perishables in boxes."

"Non-perishable? Sounds evil. And warmer places? How could it be warm somewhere else? And what is a greenhouse?" There were so many things about her world I'd yet to understand. Sounded like a fantasy, unreal and weak. They'd not dealt with the hardships we had that made us strong.

Emma smiled up at me, brushed an errant strand of hair from my forehead. "A greenhouse is a tiny house that is built for plants. It has a clear ceiling so the sun can reach the plants, but it's insulated to keep it warm."

"Clear ceiling?"

She nodded. "Glass or plastic—a synthetic material."

"Huh." I wanted to build one. Right away.

"And, there are places where the weather is different than here. You have spring, summer, fall and winter, where your weather gradually changes from warm to cold and back again. There are places in the world where it is warm all the time, and places where it is cold all the time."

"Where are these places?" Emma's view of the world was amazing and I wanted to see it, to experience it the way she told me.

"It is warm all the time in the south, and on tropical islands. Cold all the time in the north, kind of like the tips of your mountains always have a bit of ice."

I grunted my acknowledgement, trying to let all of her information sink in. "'Haps ye should show cook how to build a greenhouse. I would love to eat fresh fruit in winter."

Emma frowned, wrinkling up her pert little nose. I leaned down, kissed the tip of it.

"I could try, but truth be told, I don't know much about greenhouses, or designing a building."

"I'll send for a master builder."

She shrugged. "I guess it couldn't hurt to try."

"And then ye'd have a nice project to work on."

Her interest suddenly flared into irritation. I could see the sudden shift in her eyes before she pushed it aside.

"What is it?" I asked.

"You're trying to give me hobbies. Keep me busy. Why?" She sounded suspicious.

"I am not trying to divert ye, lass. Ye mentioned yourself that ye enjoyed gardening. I'm but giving ye a way to do it every day, if ye like."

Still, she frowned. She looked so adorable. Marred brow, flushed red cheeks, pouty lips and her red hair wild from where I'd threaded my fingers into it while we made love.

"I promise there is nothing untoward about my suggestion," I said, leaning forward and nuzzling her neck. She smelled delicious, and my cock responded, lifting and nudging her thigh.

Emma sighed, shifting her thigh back and forth, making me hot for her all over again. "All right," she murmured.

I trailed a finger down her arm, swirling in the crook of her elbow. "A lady of the castle often has projects that make the castle a better place. My mother loved to sew tapestries. Her mother before that made cushions and blankets. Many of those items still grace the chambers of Gealach today. But ye, what will ye do?"

She raised an impertinent brow. "I'm not mistress of the castle."

"Not, yet. But ye will be." I pressed my palms to her cheeks and kissed her thoroughly, pulling back only with regret. "Now, I must be off. Ewan is most likely waiting in my solar for me."

"I'll go and see Cook," Emma said, her voice showing a bit more enthusiasm than before.

I gripped her by the hand and we stepped to her chamber door, glancing up and down the corridor before exiting. "All clear," I murmured.

Sadly, we had to look before leaving any room in hopes of catching spies and would-be attackers.

"Not really," Emma said.

I turned to see that she watched Isabella making her way toward us from the opposite end of the corridor.

Coldness settled around my heart. Every bit of warmth and happiness I'd found inside the room with Emma was leached from me in the moment I met Lady Isabella's eyes. She was a ruthless woman. Calculating, and from the triumphant look on her face, she was confident she'd already won.

I gritted my teeth. "Damn."

CHAPTER THREE

Emma

*M*y heart leapt into my throat, choking me.

Slow suffocation by nerves and hate.

I tugged my hand from Logan's, observing the triumphant smirk on Isabella's face. My fingers automatically curled into a fist I longed to use and knew all too well, I'd never be allowed to.

What did she have to be triumphant about? That she'd caught us? At this point, who gave a shit if she knew?

I swallowed, feeling Logan stiffen beside me, as bunched up and tense as I was. I forced my face to remain placid, certain every thought raced over my features. I never wanted to reveal myself to her.

"There ye are, Logan," Isabella purred. The heels of her slippers clicked softly on the floor, muting as she walked over a tapestry rug. The jewels on her gown glinted in the torchlight as did the ones dripping from her ears and neck.

Logan grunted.

"I've been looking for you since ye were not outside to wish our king well." Her glossy hair swayed softly, seductively as she came to a stop in front of us. If I didn't hate her, I might be mesmerized by her. She was beautiful, elegant, the very picture of what young girls who dressed up for tea parties wanted to emulate—all except her cruel and sad heart.

"We spoke before he departed. Did ye need something?" Logan's tone was brusque, dismissive.

I couldn't help feeling a little triumphant myself, and hid the smile that inched up the corner of my lip with a little frown. Isabella's confidence swayed physically, her face as open as a book—as open as mine had been moments before. The corner of her eye twitched as did her lip as she flicked her gaze at me for a split-second before turning back to Logan.

"Aye, there is something I need." The book of her emotions closed, and the ice queen returned. I would like to ride the grounds. I thought mayhap it best if I were to ride with ye. I'd get a better account of everything if ye were to show me." Her voice ended on a suffocating purr.

Why did women feel the need to lure men in with seductive voice changes? Made me feel a little less feminine, though I shouldn't be. Logan was attracted to me because I was me. Because I wasn't afraid to show my true colors, and because I didn't tempt him with fantasies—other than ones I was willing to see met out.

Logan shook his head. "No one leaves Gealach walls."

Isabella looked taken aback. No doubt the tart had wanted to get Logan alone. I could only imagine what she had up her sleeve. I'd told her before that Logan enjoyed the company of pigs in bed—he didn't, but it had been the only thing I could think of at the spur of the moment to turn her off. I wouldn't be surprised in her haste to ensnare him if she didn't have a whole slew of piggies waiting in her chamber. I bit the inside of my cheek to keep from laughing at the image that brought to mind.

Isabella scoffed, cocking her head to the side, a delicate hand resting impudently on her hip. "Not leave the walls? That's absurd. Ye canna expect me to remain within."

Logan tilted his head, gave her the look I'd seen him make toward someone he thought might be a bit on the witless side.

"Lady Isabella, there is no one forcing ye to remain." He swept his hand toward the stairs. "Ye are free to leave Gealach whenever ye please. But ye canna return. If it pleases, I will even provide ye escort all the way back north."

Her mouth fell open, but she quickly recovered, switching back to seductress. She batted her lashes, cocked her shoulder showing off how silky her skin was, how her plush breasts could easily spill from her gown at that angle. The way she opened her eyes a little wider, giving Logan a doe-eyed gaze, made me nervous. The bitch was good. Damn good. I wouldn't be surprised if she got what she wanted every time.

"Oh, darling, dinna be angry with me. I dinna want to go home. I simply wanted to get to know your lands, your clan." She didn't need to add that they would one day be hers, it was evident, dripping from every word. She stared past Logan, and at me, her eyes dark with venom. Isabella wanted to make sure *I* understood she intended to win.

I kept my face as blank as I could—the look I used to use with my ex-husband or his mother when either of them berated me. I wouldn't show her that her words and actions stung. That would only mean she'd won, and there was no way in hell this bitch was going to steal away my man.

Logan was silent for a moment as he observed Isabella, but when he did finally speak, his voice was low and chilling. "Dinna play coy, Lady Isabella. I know why ye're here. Ye will not leave these walls unless it is to return to your people."

Sharp pain stung from my palms as my nails dug in. I wanted him to say, *when*, not *unless*. Wanted to grab his arm, shake him and hiss my need, but I didn't. I stood still as a statue, hoping and praying that all of this was a bad dream and I'd wake up cozy in Logan's arms.

Lady Isabella glared at Logan, all coyness gone, replaced by the she-devil who'd confronted me the week prior, threatening to have me whipped if I touched him. Warning that she'd have me branded a whore in front of the whole clan. I didn't doubt that she might try. I had no power in this place, except what power Logan gave me. I'd made friends, but in the end, I was the outsider. More so than Lady Isabella, for she was actually Scottish. Kin and country meant everything to the people here. A wanderer from the new world could never be embraced as much as a fellow countryman or woman.

Isabella was a noble-born lady. Her uncle a powerful man, and she had the ear of the king. I was quickly learning that being Logan's lover left me only close to the bottom of the barrel with no hopes of having any sort of power to climb out. Knowledge that left me cold, fingers numb.

The woman straightened her back, not to be cowed by Logan, though if she knew him well, she would have simply nodded and walked away. Anyone daring to challenge the master of Gealach would have hell to pay.

She licked her lips, a move meant to entice, and I couldn't have been more happy with Logan's lack of reaction. I flicked my gaze to the hand on her hip, watched as her nails dug a little harder into her gown. She, too, was trying to hide her anger.

With a toss of her head, she spoke dismissively, the hint of caution not at all concealed. "The king wishes me to remain, my laird. I but obey the edicts of my sovereign. 'Twould be dangerous, deadly, to go against King James."

Dear Lord, the vixen was insinuating that Logan was treasonous. Even I picked up on that. A serious accusation. One that could end up with him getting executed. A chill rushed over my skin. A dark sense of foreboding. This was not good.

Logan shifted away from me, stepping forward so that he was nearly nose to nose with Isabella. She was tall, taller than me, and her eyes were at his chin-level. She tilted her head back to look up at him, a flash—less than a second—of fear in her eyes.

"Dinna threaten me, Lady Isabella. Dinna dare." He spoke through his teeth, a guttural sound that had goosebumps rising on my arms. Murderous.

Isabella took a step back and Logan stepped around her heading toward the stairs. But he stopped halfway, perhaps realizing he'd left me alone with the lioness who looked ready to rip me to shreds. I could take her. I'd learned a lot in these past months. The insecure woman I'd been before was long gone. If Isabella wanted a fight, I'd plenty of pent up anger to unleash on her.

"Emma, Cook has requested your presence."

Isabella lifted her chin, giving me a look that made me want to slap her. If the bitch made it through the week without me backhanding her, we'd both be lucky.

I nodded toward Logan, expecting him to walk with me down the stairs, but he remained rooted in place. When I stared at him expectantly, he dismissed me with a nod of his head toward the stairs.

I couldn't deny the twist in my gut, the feeling of loss, jealousy, anger, all of them jumbling up inside me. He was going to stay behind with *her*, and send me to the kitchens. Lady Isabella wouldn't be caught dead in the kitchens.

I whirled toward the stairs, unable to watch as Isabella sidled up to Logan. I knew he wouldn't give in, that he wasn't going to agree. I blew out a breath as I took the stairs as quickly as I could. At least, I thought I knew he wouldn't.

He swore he'd go to the king again, that he'd never marry Isabella. But… The king was the king and his word law.

At that moment, I wished we'd been in present day instead of the sixteenth century. In modern times, it wouldn't have mattered. He could have ridden off into the sunset with me. And in modern times his king wouldn't have asked for him to marry the enemy. His castle wouldn't be attacked nearly daily either by those who wished to discover the secrets of Gealach or take down the Guardian of Scotland.

Didn't his position warrant a say in his future? Despite the fact that he was the secret brother of the king, as the Guardian, he should be able to choose his wife, or at least implore the king to choose another.

Marrying Isabella would be taking *keep your enemies close* to the extreme.

So deep in thought, I didn't see Ewan and ran smack into him at the bottom of the stairs, my nose jabbing into the pin that held his plaid in place. He steadied me, hands gripping my upper arms.

With a raised brow, he said, "Everything all right?"

Logan's second-in-command was a handsome devil. Intuitive, and had given me his shoulder to lean on a few times since I'd been there. He resembled the brother I'd lost in a plane accident a decade before, in such an uncanny way, it gave me chills every time I looked at him.

"Not really," I confessed.

"What is it?" He held up his finger, pretending to be deep in thought. "Wait, let me guess. Is it a person?"

I nodded, trying to hide my smile.

Ewan pursed his lips. "A woman?"

I rolled my eyes and nodded again.

"Does her name begin with an I?"

I smacked his arm and let out a little laugh. "You know exactly who it is, Ewan. Don't play games with me."

He chuckled. "Only trying to lighten your mood. Where are ye headed?"

"To the gardens to help with picking and other womanly duties." I couldn't help the sarcasm that dripped from every word.

"Womanly duties? I've never heard ye describe gardening in such a way before." He steered me through the great hall. "Is it because of *the* woman?"

I stopped and faced him. "Do you think—" I couldn't finish. Couldn't ask Ewan. He wouldn't know the answer and he rarely, if ever, talked about his laird's choices.

"I think ye'd do best to steer clear of her."

I nodded. "Good advice."

Ewan stepped closer and spoke in low tones. "I dinna know her well, but her family is dangerous, so I'm inclined to believe she is dangerous."

I frowned. "Has the security alert increased?"

Ewan raised a questioning brow. "If ye're talking about reinforcements, aye. We've had to with her here. The lady could decide to find a way for her uncle to gain entrance."

"You don't trust her," I stated.

"No one does." The way he said it, as though it were common knowledge, was a comfort to me.

Maybe I wasn't as alone as I thought I was.

I chewed my lip and glanced toward the doors to the kitchens. "What am I supposed to do?"

Ewan was silent for a moment, and then he said, "I think ye should just go about your day. Do the things ye normally do. When faced with a situation ye canna change, ye must adapt."

Not comforting in the least. I wanted to change the situation. Wanted to change Isabella's location. Not adapt to it all. I lifted my chin. "Sometimes, we have to make our own fate."

"And sometimes, we have to let fate lead us." Ewan looked serious as he studied me.

"Huh." I patted Ewan's arm and forced a smile. "Thanks for the pep talk."

"Pep?"

"Never mind." I left Ewan in the great hall and made my way toward the kitchens.

Walking through the kitchens, the scent of bread baking and stew simmering normally would have made my mouth water, but not today. I was still too nauseated from my encounter with Isabella. I smiled at the women chopping carrots and onions, kneading dough and stirring up concoctions in bowls, as I made my way to the back door and into the gardens, more disturbed now than I'd been before talking to Ewan.

When I was tossed back in time, I'd made the best of it — okay, more than made the best of it. I loved being here with Logan. Yes, I missed modern conveniences, like showers, Starbucks, soft toilet paper and condoms, but I was willing to give those things up in order to be with him. Willing to offer my advice — albeit in a concealed sort of way — on ways to do things better, such as the green house, or washing hands and covering one's mouth when coughing.

The sun was out, defying the chill the wind that blew at a brisk pace. I closed my eyes for a moment and took a deep breath of fresh air. I'd thought Scotland's scent was clean and fresh even in modern times, but five hundred years in the past, it was even better. Almost like breathing in one breath could heal any ailment.

The chattering of the clanswomen broke my short interlude. A dozen or more of them were bent over the last of the garden crops to be harvested, their hands covered in dirt, baskets full of radishes, carrots and other root vegetables.

"There ye are," Cook said, a frown on her face as she approached. Her hair fell around her face in gray batches from her bun and a smear of dirt spread across her nose. "We'd gotten used to your help and we thought now that a lady had arrived ye'd be up visiting with her instead of down here with us."

I smiled at her and took the basket. "You've no reason to fear me not coming to help. No matter who is visiting, I'm always willing to do my part. Besides," I said, "I really do enjoy your company, too."

Cook frowned, she'd not said she enjoyed my company, but I knew that was what she meant. The woman was hard, well-worked, but beneath her bluster, she had a big heart.

"Well, get on with it then. Onions need to be picked."

"With pleasure."

I headed toward the rows of onions, and bent down, ready to dig in the dirt for the thick bulbs. The woman beside me, nudged me with her elbow.

"That's the laird's betrothed, that woman, is it not?"

How to answer? I shrugged.

"'Tis. I heard her say so this morning after Mass."

I didn't want to sound like a jealous wench, or lay claim to the laird. Our relationship was a quiet one. We knew the clan suspected, but neither of us had come right out and said it openly.

"I hadn't heard it was official." I pulled a white bulb from the ground and stuffed it in my basket.

"She says 'tis only a matter of time."

"Hmm." I did not want to be having this conversation. At all.

"Whoever ends up married to him will be a lucky woman," she sighed, then cleared her thought. "Of course, I only hope that we're lucky in gaining a mistress."

"I'm sure his lairdship will do what's best for all of you." God, I hoped he did—and that what was best was me.

"Or what the king orders," the woman answered, sounding almost as depressed as I felt.

Another dreadful reminder that I may not have a choice in this future after all.

I tucked another onion in my basket, pretending my eyes were watering from their scent and not because I felt like I was once again floundering with no place to belong.

CHAPTER FOUR

Logan

With Emma out of earshot I took two menacing steps toward Isabella, closing the distance between us. The scent of her perfume assaulted me—strong and spicy. I found my nose offended when I'd gained so much pleasure from the light, floral scents of Emma.

"I knew ye'd come around," she purred, reaching out and sliding a manicured nail down the length of my arm.

I jerked away in reaction, gritting my teeth.

I wanted to throttle her. Wanted to take her by the upper arms and shake the life from her. Without a doubt, I knew that if I touched her, I would end up doing damage, so I kept my fists clenched at my sides.

"Ye know nothing. Stay away from Emma," I growled.

A flash of fear sparked in her dark eyes, but she masked it before I had a chance to truly examine it. "Oh, darling, ye couldn't possibly—"

I grunted. "Dinna use your feminine wiles on me. They have no place here, and I've no use for them."

She pouted, going for sultry, but it only made me think of a spoiled brat. How many men had she won over with her ploys? How many suffered?

"Logan—"

"Laird," I interrupted her, wanting to take her down a notch or two. "I've not given ye leave to be so informal."

"But we are to be married," she whined and gave a slight stomp of her foot.

"Nay, my lady, we are not." I kept my voice level and serious.

"The king says—"

"King James says a lot of things. Think ye are the first to have been brought here?" I questioned, venom dripping from each word, as I leaned closer to her face, letting her know just how damn serious I was. "Think there are not many who have walked this path before ye? And yet I remain a bachelor."

She swallowed, searching my eyes for the truth, and she'd find it there, for certain she would, because I let it shine through.

"This time will be no different," I said, lips curling into a cruel grin.

There was one difference—I'd never had to deal with a woman before like I did with Isabella. Never had to be so mean-spirited.

The woman had the nerve to raise her chin, her shoulders straightening. "Ye're so confident. So sure of yourself," she spat, fire blazing daggers from her eyes. "Ye may be the Guardian of Scotland, the bearer of some great secrets, but ye're also a man. A man who has to obey his sovereign like the rest of us."

"Aye," I drawled out.

"Your sovereign says ye'll be married to me."

I narrowed my eyes studying her. She could have been beautiful if she weren't such a cold-hearted bitch. There was something about this woman that made the hair on the back of my neck stand on end. She was cunning, but she was also a permanent resident of MacDonald's pocket, and that man wanted me dead.

"I see no contract, my lady. The king has left Gealach. He's left ye here. And he did not leave any betrothal documents behind."

She blanched, her face going whiter than the snow that was likely to fall in the next couple of weeks. "He will return," she said quickly.

"Aye." I shrugged. "But when? Sometimes months, years go by between his visits."

Her mouth fell open and she slammed it closed, bristling beneath the surface. It wouldn't be too long before the real Lady Isabella revealed herself. Her body grew rigid, and she stared up at me with as much venom as I'd seen in her uncle when he'd glared at me from within my dungeon walls before he broke free. Her eyes, they were similar to his, and come to think of it, she looked more like MacDonald than I'd thought. I wouldn't be surprised at all to find out that Lady Isabella wasn't a niece of MacDonald's at all, but a daughter. The bastard had been trying for years to get me to marry one of them, uniting us. But I knew the true reasons for his offer—he wanted my position so he could slay the king.

And he would go about any means doing it—even if it meant using his own flesh and blood.

A flood of pity filled my gut. The lass standing so stoic and vicious before me was nothing more than a pawn. Used by her family to gain what they needed, wanted.

"What do ye want, Isabella?" I asked her with all sincerity knowing full well, whatever answer I got was going to be far from the truth.

"To do my duty."

I sighed. It was a lost cause, and I couldn't waste my anger on her, there was much to do. "We all have duties, my lady, but we all also have choices." Something I'd learned from Emma. She'd struggled with choice for the majority of her adult life. Emma had revealed to me that we were all products of our choices, for even when it seemed we weren't in charge of our lives, we still had choices we could make within those bounds. Emma was intelligent, with a heart that was bigger than life itself, and when she'd arrived, she'd been so frail. Beaten down and told she was worthless. I knew better from the start, there was something inside that told me she was special. Beyond the intense urge I had to spread her thighs, I respected her so much, loved her beyond measure.

Isabella scoffed, crossing her arms over her chest. "Choice is a word men use. Women have no use for it."

"Sounds as though ye've been listening to too many ignorant men."

"I should take offense to that."

"If it pleases."

She glared at me. "Why do ye speak to me this way?"

"What way?" I backed off, no longer needing to threaten her or invade her space, at least not at the moment.

"Ye were cold to me afore, and now ye're being..." She chewed her lip. "'Tis a trick?"

Good God, had no one ever been nice to her before?

"'Haps ye will come to find out in life that not everything is always so black and white," I said. "Sometimes, there can be a middle ground."

"To what are ye referring? If ye're speaking of our marriage, then there is no gray, nor is there black or white. There is only one color—the king's will."

"Ye are that loyal to King James?"

"Why shouldn't I be?" That flicker of fear reared in her eyes once more.

"Need I spell it out?"

"Suppose ye do."

"Ye're a MacDonald, my lady."

"And my uncle is very close to the king."

"Aye, but is he loyal?"

"How dare ye question his loyalty!" Whatever wall she'd dropped a moment ago was racked back up and this time with barbs as she thrust herself toward me in a move that might have been menacing if she was closer to my size.

"'Tis a question that begs an answer."

"I *and* my family are most loyal to the crown."

Lady Isabella was a lot more clever than I gave her credit for before. Indeed, she was a pawn, but her thoughts may have been so darkened that she may never come back to the light. She never mentioned James' name, only king and crown. And MacDonald believed himself to be entitled to both of those.

"Seems 'twas my mistake," I said with a quick bow. "Will not happen again." I backed away a couple of feet and swept my arm toward the stairwell. "After ye, my lady. I've many duties to complete today."

She humphed, raising her chin even higher as she gave a wide skirt around me.

"Mistake, indeed. See that it doesna happen again. Often wolves hide in sheep's clothing. One would not want to mistake ye for a traitor, *my laird*. And to be clear, if need be, King James made it clear he would be happy to take that whore off your hands."

The viper was back. I reached for her, grasping her arm just above the elbow and pressing on the spot there that would make her arm tingle uncomfortably. "Mind your tongue," I ground out.

She tried to wrench free, but I didn't let go. If she wanted to voice threats, best she understood who held the upper hand.

"Mind your tongue," I repeated, slower this time.

Isabella opened her mouth to reply, but bit the tip of her tongue instead. What vile words was she about to hiss?

I let go of her, glaring fiercely. "On with ye, now."

She grumbled, whirled away and lifted her skirts higher than was necessary as she took to the stairs, revealing black-knit hose that if I'd seen them on Emma, I might have dragged her back upstairs. Mayhap that was the woman's intention, to entice me.

She'd be in for a rude awakening, as I was not to be enticed by anyone but Emma. Only she could quench my thirst. Only she could move me in ways I never thought possible.

I listened until the sound of Isabella's slippers on the stairs disappeared, then I returned to both our doors, making sure they were locked. Isabella had revealed much during our short exchange, especially that she was not to be trusted. Sent here, no doubt on a mission, to discover the secrets, or at the very least to marry me to bide her time in finding them. Marrying me also gave her uncle access to me. Not that I would grant it—if for some unearthly reason I did marry her. Nay, not in this lifetime, the next, or eternity would I say vows with that woman.

I whirled on the nearest wall and crashed my fist into it, pain radiating up my arm as my knuckles split against the stone. A roar of anger, frustration, pain ripped from my throat. I stared up at the ceiling, not seeing it, chest puffing, heart pounding.

From the moment James had crossed my threshold gifting me with the news of our blood ties and offering protection in exchange for his own, my life had not been my own. I was utterly out of control as much as I wanted, needed to govern my own destiny. At every turn, some new intrigue gave birth to itself. Not a moment of peace, except for when I was in Emma's arms and now he wished to wrench that from me as well.

I stormed down the stairs. No place in mind that I was to go, but knowing I couldn't stand there any longer, not with the stench of Isabella's bitterness and my own brother's betrayal so ripe in the air.

And then I was there, without realizing my intent, the hidden alcove that stared out onto the gardens. I slipped inside the narrow, darkened recess and sat on the stone bench in order to see out the thin slit in the two foot thick walls. The gardens were filled with clanswomen working, and I looked from one to the other until my eyes caught the glimmer of fiery hair.

Emma.

She was crouched before a patch and rooted through the dirt, upending what looked to be onions. I swelled with pride watching her, seeing how those around her looked on her with respect and even something akin to friendship. She'd found her place here, even if she lamented often that she didn't think she had. My people loved her, just as I did.

They would want her for their mistress, I was sure of it. I watched her swipe at her face as she went. Tears brought on by irritation from the onions, or some other aggravation?

My heart pulsed harder, and the keen urge to rush outside and pull her into my arms, demanding who had done her wrong was powerful. And I would have done it, too, if it weren't for several reasons, one being that I was fairly certain her frustration with Isabella was the reason behind her tears and I had no answer for her there. I was just as frustrated.

My conversation with the traitorous witch had gone nowhere. I didn't want to speak to Emma about it until I could offer her some measure of comfort. With one last longing look in her direction, I left the alcove in search of Ewan.

One thing was for certain, Isabella's presence only meant imminent danger to the clan. We needed extra lookouts and the dear wench needed a body guard — or rather a spy — to relay all her dealings to me.

There was no way in hell she as going to win. I am the Guardian of Scotland. I guard the king's secrets and I guard them well.

And damn if I was going to let anyone take Emma away from me. They'd have to claw through my dead body and then my devil spirit before they did. I would remain victorious.

CHAPTER FIVE

Emma

*T*he hair on the back of my neck prickled, stood on end. Dirt covered the tip of my nose as I scratched it a half a dozen times trying to get rid of the incessant tickle. Signs. All signs of someone watching me. That was, if I believed in superstition. An ominous feeling churned in my gut. I believed all right.

After traveling five-hundred years back in time, I was liable to believe anything. Given the number of threats made against myself and Logan since I arrived, it would probably be smart if I did trust my body's warnings.

I dusted my hands of dirt and stood, turning in a circle slowly as I observed those in the garden. The same clanswomen I worked with each and every day labored tirelessly. Some bent over in the dirt as I'd been, others carrying baskets. A couple of the castle dogs wandered in the pathways, getting pats from a few and swats from others. Nothing appeared to be out of the ordinary. There were no strangers—no Lady Isabella, in particular.

So why did it feel like I was—

There—in the shadows by the wall, near the gate where a path led from the gardens to the inner bailey at the front of the castle stood a figure in shadows. The sun glinted in just the right way so I couldn't see who it was—but I had a good idea.

Isabella.

So she was there after all. Damn.

I put my hands over my eyes, shading the sun and the outline of her gown came into view. She was spying on me, quite obviously. She made no move to leave after I'd seen her. A shiver stole down my spine, curling its way around my middle. For some reason, I feared her presence more than I'd feared anyone else's the entire time I'd been there. More than the men who attacked the castle on numerous occasions. More than the king who wished to take me to his bed. More than the dark and cold shifts of air in the secret chamber buried fifty feet below the castle. This woman stood for all that could undo me.

She had the king's blessing. She had the backing of her evil, powerful uncle. She knew more about this country, this castle, the workings of society than I did, and she was playing by society's rules.

I was a harlot in her eyes, and she meant to dispose of me. Question was, would she win?

I frowned and removed my hand from shading my eyes. I couldn't let her win, but I needed some way to push her out. Some way to win this silent battle.

"What's got ye looking so stern?" Cook said as she sidled up to me.

I glanced at her, watching her stiffen as she saw where I looked. But when I looked back, Isabella was gone and the gate was shifting closed.

"Her, I see," Cook said.

"Yes. Her."

"Dinna fash about her, lass. The laird willna take her to wed."

I cocked my head, suddenly interested. "Why do you say that?"

"She's kin of the MacDonald of course."

I was a little disappointed at her answer, hoping she would have given me more than that. Like maybe I was better, or Isabella sucked ass. I nodded. "Does that matter if the king has decided they should be married?"

Cook grunted in disgust. "Dinna underestimate his lairdship. He's often led the king away from disaster. He but needs to coddle the man a bit more." She turned away from the gate and met my eyes, her expression thoughtful. I'd never seen her this way before. Cook was all about orders and people doing what she told them. Now it appeared she looked at me as though we were friends. "He'll need all the support he can get, my lady, if ye know my meaning."

I thought I did, but one never knew when dealing with people five hundred years in the past. Some things seemed to get lost in the translation. "I'm not sure I do."

"Might I speak out of turn?" she asked, sidling closer so that no one could overhear us.

"Of course," I said, keeping my voice just as hushed as hers.

"Ye love Laird Grant, do ye nay?"

I swallowed, frowning and crossing my arms over my chest. "I suppose I've been more obvious about it than I thought."

"We can all see it in the way ye look at him." She smiled. "He is a mighty fine warrior."

"That he is." I nodded.

"If ye love him, dinna let him go."

I smoothed out my apron, though there wasn't a wrinkle in it. "I'm not sure I'll have a choice in the matter. King's wishes and all."

"Well, now," she scoffed. "If we all thought that way, what a sorry mess we'd be. Show him what ye have to offer. Prove to him that he'll be better for it. Sometimes a man needs a swift kick in the arse to move forward with what is right. They like to mull it over. Seems the only time I've ever seen a man jump to do anything was when they were threatened by the enemy face to face."

A soft chuckle escaped me. My arms fell to my sides. "I guess they like to make sure when they finally act that they've made the right decisions."

"Behind every man who's made the right choice is a woman who made the choice for him. If he's in the wrong, he likely came up with the idea himself." Cook nodded as if her words were fact—and I couldn't help laughing in turn.

"Cook!" I couldn't believe what she was saying. I had a lot more confidence in Logan than that. He was smart, tactical, loyal, sensual, caring... Oh, I could wax on about him all day, but that wasn't going to do me any good. "Logan—I mean, Laird Grant, is extremely intelligent."

The woman looked suddenly contrite. "I meant no disrespect, honest. I was but suggesting ye push him along in making his decision to confront... ye know who," she ended on a whisper behind her hand.

Judging from the way Cook shifted on her feet and was suddenly wringing her hands I had a good idea I'd made her nervous, and now she felt she couldn't speak freely.

I reached out and placed a hand on her shoulder. Sending her a friendly smile, I said, "I do greatly appreciate your advice, and trust me, I will take it to heart. I need to talk to him about this situation. He needs to make it right for the clan, and I pray he'll choose the best option."

"Which is ye." Cook looked back to her old self.

I smiled, hating seeing that sudden break in her smile. "I think so."

She smiled back at me. "Good. Now finish up with those onions and quit looking off into the distance like ye think your life is over."

I flopped onto the chair in my room, back a bit sore from bending over for hours in the garden and then trekking basket upon heavy basket into the castle and down the cellar stairs. No wonder the women of the Highlands were so robust. Every muscle ached.

There was a soft knock at the door and then Agatha popped her head in. Damn, I'd forgotten to lock the door. I needed to get into the habit of doing that...

"Cook said ye might like a bath, my lady."

The thought of submerging my sore body into a tub of steamy water almost had me crying out Hallelujah. I nodded and smiled. "Thank ye."

She opened the door wide and servants rushed in with a wooden tub, buckets of steamy water and all the supplies I'd need to wash. After the bath was set up, Agatha started to help me undress, but I brushed her hands aside.

"If you don't mind, I'd like to be alone," I said.

Agatha gave me an odd look. "But, my lady —"

"Please."

She bowed her head. "Some wine, then."

It was her job to serve as my maid, and I was grateful to have her, but sometimes, being fawned over, was a little much. And I wanted to enjoy the peace and relaxation of the bath without having to chatter with Agatha who loved to talk my ear off. I wanted to wash my own hair. I used to love going to the salon and having my hair washed and blow dried, but now... Now it was a task that had been taken away from me, and there was enough things taken already.

I nodded and she poured me a glass, handing it to me on her way to the door.

"Call out for me if ye're in need, my lady. I'll be just beyond the door."

I shook my head. "I can't stand the idea of you just sitting outside my door. Why not go do something for yourself for the next hour or so and then come back?"

Agatha looked as though I'd asked her to climb to the top of the battlements and leap off.

"Go on. That's an order."

A twinkle came into her eyes. "Well now, lass, if 'tis an order, I just may go and rest my feet a bit."

"Good." I smiled and waved her out of the room. Following behind her, I barred the door and feeling slightly guilty for pushing her away. But, I was also pleased she'd go and have a little rest for herself. She deserved it.

I shucked my clothes, shivering at the draft that swirled around my ankles. There was a fire lit, which did a good job warming the room, but even still, nothing beat modern furnaces. The wine helped a little, but mostly just to heat my cheeks.

I hopped from foot to foot, the wooden planks of the floorboards like ice against my toes. Once I made it to the tub, I nearly leapt into the warm water—a stark contrast to the temperature of the room.

Sinking down into the steamy bath, I closed my eyes and let the water cover my ears, until the world ceased to exist. Black behind my eyes, and silence in the water. I could imagine that I was anywhere, anyone. And yet, I imagined being here at Gealach and that I was myself. I smiled, realizing that for the first time, I was proud to be me. I'd finally found a place I belonged. Funny—and sad—that it was five hundred years in the past. I should have been born in another time.

With a sigh of resignation, I sat up in the tub and grabbed the bar of soap Agatha left. It smelled of lavender this time. The clan made their own soaps, and every time a different scent was used. The last one had been rosemary, and while it was a heavenly scent, I couldn't help but feel a little like I was preparing myself for the oven like a turkey.

Using the linen washcloth, I soaped it up and then washed the grime of the garden from my hands, and arms, cleansing myself in both mind and body. The lavender was calming.

A few swift taps came from the sliding door that connected my bedroom to Logan's, and then it slid open, revealing his brawny figure to me.

"Emma—" He stopped suddenly on an indrawn breath, eyes darkening as he watched me, one arm suspended in mid-air as I washed it.

"Hello," I said, pretending that I hadn't noticed the sudden, intense desire that filled his features. I continued to circle soap on my arm drawing closer to my shoulders and breasts.

"Ye're in the bath."

I pressed my lips together to hold in a laugh. "Yes. I was filthy from gardening."

He stepped into the room and slid the door closed between our chambers. Without a word he grabbed one of my chairs and slid it over to the tub, stopping behind me. I heard the creek of the chair as he sat in it, and then his hands were on my hair, his fingers threading trenches.

"Ye've such beautiful hair. Soft and silky and as fiery as your passion." I felt his mouth near my ear, his breath tickling my skin and sending skitters of chills up and down my limbs. "Let me wash it?"

A smiled flashed on my lips. I'd just dismissed Agatha in favor of washing my own hair, but the idea of Logan doing it… Well, I couldn't pass up the offer.

"Yes." I leaned my head back into his palms.

He gently laid my head on the rim of the tub, then leaned over me to cup his hands in the water. Droplets seeped from between his hands, falling onto my chest, my lips, my forehead. I felt each of those drops as intimately as if they'd been kisses. He parted his hands over my head, water sluicing over my hair, and I let out a long sigh. Logan washing my hair felt more intimate than even some of our embraces. Logan repeated the process again and again until my hair was thoroughly wet to his satisfaction. Seeing as how I'd already submerged in the water, I think he rather liked the way the water sluiced over my hair down my face and over my breasts. I think he liked to watch every line of water drip. And I thoroughly loved it, thrusting my chest upward to improve his view.

"Hand me the soap, love."

I reached up and handed him the lavender bar. His fingers brushed mine, sliding sensually over my palm and I shuddered.

The sound of him slicking his hands with soap sent greedy spirals of anticipation skidding over me, and then his fingers were sliding through my hair again. He massaged against my scalp in circles, hitting every pressure point that relieved stress. Did he even realize what he was doing?

I moaned, letting myself sink further into his hands.

"Dunk, love."

I slipped forward, taking a deep breath and holding it as I fell beneath the water. Logan massaged the soap from my hair until my scalp tingled along with the rest of me.

"I love the way you wash hair," I murmured as I rose from beneath the water, feeling completely relaxed, boneless.

His breath was on my ear again, making my breasts feel full, heavy and my nipples taut, aching for him to grasp them. As if reading my body's silent language, he slid his hands into the water and stroked them over my belly, the undersides of my breasts.

"Shall I wash the rest of ye, just as thoroughly?"

57

I groaned, and nodded, ready for the onslaught of pleasure that was about to come my way.

CHAPTER SIX

Emma

Slick, sensual hands rubbed up the length of my torso, teasing over my sensitive nipples, before escaping and leaving me wanting.

"What will you teach me this time?" I asked, growing bold with each of our encounters. I barely remembered the shy, shell of myself that I'd been when I first arrived.

Logan chuckled, the raw sound near my ear sending my nerves into tingling spasms.

"Ye're always so eager to learn."

I nodded, not even trying to deny it.

"Hmm," he said, pinching each of my nipples as he tugged gently on my earlobe with his teeth. "Mayhap this time I want to watch ye pleasure yourself while ye pleasure me."

My insides clenched, a spark of decadence erupting in my sex with each word. I was immediately interested.

"Show me," I demanded.

Logan disappeared for a moment into his chamber, returning with a small, red velvet bag. He grinned wickedly at me and my heart skipped a beat, tongue went dry. What was in the bag?

"With this," he said. He opened the bag, pulling out something I'd never expected to see in this era—a dildo. But not just any dildo, this one was made of marble, and greatly resembled Logan's cock.

"That's..." My voice trailed off and I swallowed. I'd never used one before.

"Modeled after my own," he murmured. "The king sent a man, along with many other...presents... to produce it for me so I could use it on..."

He didn't continue, and he didn't need to. The picture of Logan with more than one woman was enough to make me fly into a jealous rage, but instead I reached out for the marble cock, and he pressed it onto my palm. It even had the same prominent vein running along the length of it.

"Wow," I whispered.

"I want to watch ye pleasure yourself with my cock, while ye pleasure my real cock."

I nodded, tongue too tied to answer. Suddenly I was hot all over, and not just from the warmth of the water.

Logan walked back behind me and lifted my head, then laid it back down on the edge of the tub, having placed a rolled towel there. "Lean back and look at me."

I leaned my head all the way back, the soft towel a nice cushion against the edge of the tub. I looked up at him as he stood. His knees were near my head and his kilt played peek-a-boo with my senses, I could almost make out the lines of his hardened cock.

He smiled down at me. "A perfect position."

For what? I wanted to ask, but my breath had hitched and I felt that any words able to make it past the tightening of my throat would only sound like gibberish.

Logan stripped off his clothes, revealing inch after inch of hardened sinew, until he stood bare above me. His thighs clenched, cock hard, abs flat and ridged. He bent over, putting his hands on the edges of the tub, his long, thick cock just barely touching my lips.

"Touch yourself," he ordered. "Put the cock inside ye."

I nodded, even though he couldn't see me. My knees fell open, ready, excited, and I dragged the dildo slowly over my abdomen toward the juncture of my thighs. The other went up to clutch a breast. I slid my fingers between the folds of my sex, feeling how slick I was already, not from the water, but from the desire Logan elicited from me. The excitement and allure of something new. I pressed the head of the dildo toward my opening, stroking it softly over my clit and shuddering at its hard, cold form—but liking it. The pad of my finger brushed over my sensitive clit and I bounced a little in the water, not expecting the shock it gave me. I was a lot more turned on that I'd thought.

"That's it, lass, let me see ye push it inside ye."

With the head positioned at my opening, I parted my thighs more and pushed it in an inch, feeling my body stretch to the demands of the marble. I cried out, wicked, forbidden sensations running rampant.

"Aye, lass, like that." Logan's breath hitched. "Now lick me."

I groaned, feeling myself falling into that familiar drugged state, intoxicated by the heady sound of his voice and the potent sensations taking over my mind and body.

I flicked my tongue out, running it over the length of his cock as I pressed the marble deeper still. Logan hissed a breath, and he stiffened all over, preparing himself for the onslaught of sensation, for I knew it was just as intense for him. He kept himself just out of reach, so all I could do was tease him, tease myself. Trailing my free hand downward, I stroked slowly over my clit, slackening the pumps of the marble, timing them with the movements of my tongue.

Logan growled, shifting to the side of the tub. I turned my head, now at a better angle to suck him in deep.

"Take hold of my cock. Slide the marble out." He hissed a breath as a I trailed my nails ever so lightly across the inside of his thigh. "Now put me in your mouth, and slide the marble inside ye, at the same time."

I moaned, grabbing hold of his thickness and angling him toward me. I was surprised at how moving just a few inches to the side had made it so much easier for me to pleasure him. I leaned forward a little more and placed the velvet head on my lips as I skimmed the edge of my slit with my fingers and the marble. I canted my hips forward, pushing the dildo deep inside myself as I sucked his cock into my mouth. His cockhead hit he back of my throat, and his musky male scent enticed me.

Above me, Logan cursed then groaned.

I loved when he started to unwind.

"Slow, lass, take it slow."

"Mmm," I moaned. I withdrew him slowly, sliding the marble out and swirling it over my clit, and then sucked him back in at the same time I thrust the warmed dildo inside.

It was hot and wicked. And though I tried to keep it slow, to move at a pace that wouldn't ruin us both, I couldn't help but go quicker. Desire, passion, pleasure, all demanded I propel us forward. My hands took on a mind of their own, slipping the unforgiving stone in and out, up and down. Circling over my clit, and pushing and pulling him in and out of my mouth. My tongue circled over the head of his cock, teasing the ridge. I was frantic in my need for us both to finish.

"Wait," he croaked, jerking back from me.

He came around to the side of the tub, reached into the water and lifted me out. I wrapped my legs around his waist and he took me to the bed, setting my rear down on the edge. With a wicked wink he set the marble aside and grabbed a pillow.

"Lift up, love."

I eyed the pillow with curiosity as I lifted my behind. Logan tucked the pillow beneath me and curled his lip in a sensuous way that had my sex clenching.

"The pleasure will be much more intense."

I nodded, already my breath catching at the thought. Gripping his cock, he drove it deep inside me, hitting a spot he'd not before stroked, and I cried out with pleasure and with the unmistakable difference between stone and flesh.

I leaned one hand back on the bed to balance myself and grabbed his taut ass with the other. He was right. The pleasure was excruciating. I kept my legs up around his waist, and let my head fall backward as he thrust hard and deep, his fingers digging into my hips.

Then he stilled. Motionless and buried deep.

"I want to feel ye climax around me." He leaned forward and kissed me, his tongue sliding against my own. I kissed him hungrily, desperate to reach my peak. "Touch yourself again."

I slipped my fingers back against my clit, throbbing and so damn wet. I wanted to give him what he wanted. Round and round I went, teasing myself and him. Let myself get just close enough that I was gasping before hesitating and putting off that final moment of pure ecstasy.

He kissed me some more, nibbling at my lips, his cock frozen deep inside me, and then I couldn't hold it any more. I pushed myself to the edge and shattered, my insides spasming, gripping him, fluttering, squeezing his cock. Logan growled, his fingers on my hips tightened and I knew it must have been a test of his will not to start pounding into me.

Dark Side of the Laird

Not until my orgasm subsided did he finally move once more, and I knew he was letting go of his control. He didn't drive inside me with a slow, steady pace, instead he rode me like a man dying of thirst. Hard, fast. Holding myself up with my abs, I gripped both hands tight to his ass, feeling the muscles tightened beneath my fingertips.

The sounds of our moans and the slapping of flesh echoed off the stone walls. Sounds of pleasure, of pure, raw, carnality. Potent and intoxicating.

Logan thrust deep, quaking between my thighs with the force of his orgasm. He grunted, his forehead falling to mine.

"What would I have done?" he asked.

"About what?"

"All these months long, I've been wanting, searching for what we —" A loud rap at the door interrupted him.

Logan scowled fiercely. Scary enough that I was glad I hadn't interrupted him. Whoever it was, was about to see the dark side of their laird.

"Who is it?" he said loudly through gritted teeth.

There was a pause, as if the person on the other side of the door was second guessing their plan of knocking.

Logan climbed off me and stalked toward the door, bellowing, "Who is it?"

I yanked up the covers, feeling my face flush with embarrassment. Logan wrapped his plaid around his middle, tucking in a loose edge so whoever was at the door would definitely notice he'd been disrobed moments before.

"'Tis Ewan," I heard from the other side before Logan swung it open.

"What is it?" Logan's voice was softer now, having most likely realized that Ewan would only interrupt him if it was important.

Ewan straightened himself to his full height, his hands tucked behind his back as he addressed his laird. "'Tis Lady Isabella, my laird."

"What?" Logan asked, sounding tired.

I was tired of hearing her name, too.

"The lady was found skulking around outside the forbidden corridor."

"Is she all right?" Logan asked, a frown marring his handsome features.

What could he possibly mean by that? And then I remembered the time I'd tried to find his office and I'd nearly been skewered by his sword as it thrust through a hidden slit in the wall.

Logan's office was in the forbidden corridor, a place guarded by burly looking men who weren't afraid to retaliate against unwanted guests. I'd never wandered down that hallway again unless invited, for fear of my life.

No wonder he feared for hers. We wanted her gone, not dead. A dead Lady Isabella was only bound to bring an army of MacDonald warriors down on Logan's head.

"The lady is fine. There was no threat to her physically, but she did not like being carted off. I think she may have been frightened." Ewan frowned and glanced toward the floor. "'Haps a little vengeful now."

I couldn't help but smirk. A *little* vengeful was most likely putting it nicely.

"Where is she?" Logan asked.

"In her chamber."

"What was her explanation for being there?"

"Says she got lost."

Logan grunted. "How did she lose the guards who were supposed to be watching her?"

Ewan shook his head. "That, I fear, ye will not be pleased with. They were found in the armory drunker than a lad with his first dram."

"Drunk?" Even from where I lay on the bed I could feel the sudden flare of fiery rage in Logan.

Ewan nodded. "An empty barrel of ale and two spilled mugs."

"Damn." The word was hushed, said under his breath. Logan's hands came to his hips and he shook his head, looking down toward the ground.

I had a sudden flashback of the last warrior who went against Logan. The beating he'd received was vicious, bloody and the thing of nightmares. Ewan had been the one to administer the punishment and I wondered if he, too, was remembering.

Ewan waited patiently while Logan fought within himself. I could tell it was hard for him to make the choice. To punish men he trusted.

"I just dinna understand why they would do that," Logan said. "I explicitly said they were to never leave her alone for a minute."

Ewan crossed his arms over his chest. "I canna explain it, my laird, other than what I saw plain with my own eyes."

"The situation does not sit right with me," Logan said. "The men would not blatantly disregard their orders without just cause. They are not traitors. And ale is not a big enough draw for them."

"What are ye thinking?" Ewan asked.

I tried to remain as small as I could on the bed, enjoying this back and forth and learning much in the way of Logan's mind and how it worked.

"I dinna know. Nothing," Logan said with a shake of his head. "I canna fathom the men shirking their duties, and I canna believe that they allowed the woman to get them drunk. That would be just as ridiculous as the both of them skipping their post to share a barrel."

"Aye, I canna say I disagree. The men seemed confused about it."

"No doubt they were. But if they had the barrel and were unconscious when ye found them, there is no question they may have some issues remembering." Logan let out a deep sigh. "Take them to the dungeon. They can sober up in the darkness. I'll think about how to deal with Isabella."

Ewan nodded, bowed, flashed a smile over Logan's shoulder toward me, which earned him a jealous shove from my lover. I laughed and buried myself deeper in the blankets.

Logan shut the door behind Ewan and turned to face me, his face grave. "I have to speak with Isabella. Warn her not to go snooping around. The woman will likely get herself killed and bring a war upon us."

I sat up in the bed, hugging the sheet close to me. "That's what I fear, too. She's not good for us, or for Gealach."

"Aye." Logan unraveled the plaid at his waist and began pleating it back around.

I chewed my lip, wanting to shout with frustration. Why wouldn't he do something about it then?

"When you talk to her…"

He glanced up from his pleats. "What?"

I drew in a deep breath and then let out what I was thinking in one rush of air. "How long must we wait before you implore the king? Before Isabella discovers something or tries to hurt someone?"

"She won't hurt anyone."

His male ego was irritating at the moment. "How do you know?" I asked. "She's a MacDonald, don't they do whatever it takes to get their way—no matter the costs?"

He frowned.

I leaned closer, trying to read the emotions hiding behind his fierce frown. "I'm right, aren't I?"

Logan's eyes locked on mine, fierce and powerful. "Aye, ye are."

CHAPTER SEVEN

Logan

*T*he laird's solar was cold, chilling my bones, but I had no desire to light a fire. I left the hearth bare, ash littering the floor. I liked the cold, it kept me on my toes, helped me to think. Helped my men to think and to listen. The best laid plans were hatched in this room by my men and my father before me.

After I finished speaking with my men today, I was going to have my nuisance guest brought in for questioning as well. Keeping the room chilled elicited a certain mindset from anyone I was going to interview, in this case, Lady Isabella. One of the reasons dungeons were so unpleasant — the incessant chill.

Three short taps sounded on the wooden door. Ewan. "Enter," I called.

The door opened swiftly and in strode Ewan and several of my trusted guards in charge of certain sectors — Master of the Main Gate, Master of the Water Gate and Master of the Scouts.

I nodded to them each, keeping my face devoid of emotion. They closed the door and all four of them stood facing me. Each was dressed for war as they always were—weapons adorning every inch of space on their arms, legs, back, axes on their belts.

"Men." I faced them, hands behind my back. "Ye're all aware of the king's visit and his departure. As I'm sure ye're aware that he left behind a lady he wishes me to marry."

The men gave me curt nods, none showing how they felt on the matter.

"The woman is the niece of MacDonald," I stated.

As trained, the men showed little reaction to that news. Simply kept their eyes on me.

"Obviously, I canna marry her," I continued. "For more reasons than I care to recount, but I'm certain ye can surmise why."

Again, curt nods. My men were observant.

"With Lady Isabella in the castle, we'll have to double our efforts in protecting Gealach and our surrounding lands. As far as I'm concerned, the castle now harbors an enemy." I paced in front of them. "Have ye heard of the two men I had assigned to watch over her? How they ended up drunk in the storeroom?"

Master of the Water Gate, Taig, looked stricken for a moment before resuming his control. One of the men was his brother.

I stopped in front of Taig. "Aye, your brother."

He stared at me, lips pressed firmly together, waiting. His red brows were drawn together in a frown, but he didn't speak his mind. And I knew he wouldn't without permission.

"Speak," I said.

"My laird, Baodan wouldn't do that. He takes his position very seriously. This clan is all he has. He respects ye greatly and would never want to see harm come to ye, the clan or Gealach." Taig shook his head. "I canna fathom what has transpired, but I would consider it foul play."

"And yet he's found sotted when he's supposed to be on duty? The man is so far gone, he can barely speak his name," I replied. "What explanation do ye give for this? That a slip of a woman held a funnel to his lips and forced him to consume the ale?"

Taig shook his head. "Baodan has never gotten like that before in his life." The man sounded as mystified as I felt.

"There's a first for everything." I shoved aside the immediate thoughts of Emma that blasted into mind.

So many firsts with her. So many more to have.

I walked away from Taig, centering my attention on the Master of the Scouts. "What say ye? Any more of your men going by the wayside?"

Gregor shook his head. "Nay, my laird. All are loyal and accounted for."

Month's before, a scout was found fraternizing with the enemy, allowing a trebuchet to be built in his territory and then used to take down part of our castle walls. The deed could not go unpunished. He'd been found guilty of treason and his sentence was death. No man wanted to face the angry-cat, a leather cat-o-nine tails with jagged stones at its ends. The weapon wasn't meant to keep a man alive. I frowned at the memory—of both being betrayed and having to take a man's life.

After what happened to the last scout, all the men went out of their way to show their loyalty.

"What is your report of the borders?" I asked.

"Nothing pressing, my laird. The neighboring clans are sticking to their own lands. A group of laborers were traveling along the south side of the castle, staying close to the loch. The sheep and cow herders were told to keep the animals close and not to wander up the mountains."

"In what direction did the laborers continue?"

"They were continuing south west."

"Did your scout speak with them?"

He shook his head. "Nay, my laird. They followed to see that the men continued off of Grant land, and once they were gone without incident, he returned to his post."

"And they haven't been seen since?"

"Nay, my laird."

It was entirely possible that the group of laborers were simply passing through. Could be they were looking for work, but it was also conceivable that the men were in fact MacDonald warriors in disguise. Scouting out the lay of the castle and our guards to better aid them in attack.

"Keep your men on their toes. I have a feeling we'll have guests soon. MacDonald's men know how well we fortify the castle. Gaining entry through force won't be an option for them. They will try to gain entrance through other means. Trickery. Or through assistance from someone within."

I turned to the Master of the Gate. "Ye and your men know well who comes and goes daily. Keep the gate closed at all times. No one new steps through that gate — beggar, merchant, priest — without first being assessed by ye."

I trudged over to my desk and pulled the cork from a bottle of whisky, then poured each of the men and myself a dram. I handed them the cups.

"These are uncertain times. Our king has gone to war with England once again — and he's losing. The nobles are all getting skittish. Only more incentive for MacDonald to make his move." I took a swallow of the whisky, letting it burn a path down my throat. "The northern arse is going to do all that he can to win his bid for the crown, including marrying his family to me."

Taig cleared his throat, shifting uncomfortably. He'd not taken a sip of whisky at all.

"What is it?" I asked.

"Where is Baodan? I'd like to speak with him." Anger edged the man's lips. Giving me the impression he'd like to do a lot more than simply speak with his brother. Though, I'd a sixth sense it was not directed at me.

"He's in the dungeon for the time being, Taig. Take a breath and remember your duty to this clan. Ye can deal with your brother later."

Taig met my eyes. "Ye, see, my laird, that's just it. Ye are my priority, I know that. I was but hoping I could get to the bottom of Baodan's motives. 'Haps shed some light on it."

I cracked my knuckles studying the man. Considering my only sibling was a spoiled king I couldn't get through to, it was hard for me to assess whether Taig talking to Baodan would do any good. But in the end, I relented. "Ye may go to him now." I nodded to Gregor. "Ye go with him. Hang in the shadows."

I dismissed the men and turned to Ewan. "Bring her to me."

"Lady Isabella?"

"Aye. 'Tis time her and I had an understanding."

"Aye, my laird."

Once the door was closed, I turned back to the empty hearth, staring into nothingness, but seeing so much. Emma staring at me in bed, her heady expression enough to make me hard now. She wore the black, sheer lace gown — the one that someone had so callously torn apart and left on our doorsteps months before. I'd have to see that another one was made. Then her expression changed, staring back at me was Emma with disappointment in her eyes. Damn, but I didn't want to let her down. Disappointing her would also be letting down my clan. It would mean that MacDonald had won. And that I could see, too. Burning buildings and screaming clansmen, women and children. Horse's carrying MacDonalds as they raced through the villages burning buildings and mauling children. Suffering because I'd been too much a coward to do the right thing.

With the king busily planning his next strikes on England, he'd not wanted to listen to me rant about MacDonald. As I saw it, I might have to take these matters into my own hands. Bring the fight to MacDonald. But I couldn't do so without first talking to James. At least trying once more to reason with him.

I needed some proof from Isabella. Something that I could take with me to the king to give him reason to side with me, and allow me to move forward with my plans. Proof that she was but a pawn, that she meant to honor her uncle's plans. Proof of what those plans were.

A swift knock sounded at the door. A glance through the eyehole showed Ewan and Isabella standing in the corridor. He had the woman by her elbow and though she looked contrite, the way her eyes shifted about, I could tell she was scared. Her eyes were wider than normal, mouth in an obstinate bow. Hands held tight together at her waist.

I opened the door, allowing them both entrance.

"My laird," she mumbled, glancing at a chair before the unlit hearth. I didn't offer her a place to sit, preferring she remain as uncomfortable as possible. The lady, as bold as she was, wouldn't go and take it without permission. There were some things even obstinate fools knew better than to do.

When her gaze met mine it was with barely held in fury. "Ye said I wouldn't be a prisoner here," she spat.

Judging from her stance, there was so much more she wanted to say, but the woman held her tongue, 'haps wanting to see what I had to say about it. Wanting to glean from me what I knew of her treachery. Smarter than I thought, though not as cunning.

I stalked toward her, invading her space enough to be uncomfortable but not enough to make her like it. She moved back only an inch or two, her eyes glancing down, and I wondered if she was taking in the weapons I carried or simply interested in my physique.

74

Eliza Knight

Towering over her, I said through gritted teeth, "And ye never said ye were here to skulk around in places where ye dinna belong." I flicked my gaze to Ewan and nodded my head toward the door. "That will be all, Ewan."

Ewan raised a brow but said nothing as he retreated. "I'll be just outside the door, my laird."

"'Twill not be necessary, Ewan. Please see to Lady Emma's protection."

We exchanged nods then I turned my attention back to the woman who represented my enemy in so many ways. Her hair was pulled back tight, making the skin around her temples stretch. She wore a dab of rouge on her lips and cheeks as was the fashion with ladies at court. And if she weren't so damn mean, she might have been a beauty.

"What are ye doing here?" I asked her, studying her eyes for signs of lying.

"That brute guard of yours brought me here."

Ah, so she meant to play games. I was hoping for quick and painless. "Nay, ye dinna understand my meaning, or ye ignore it. I'm asking what ye're doing in Gealach."

She lifted her chin, showing the haughty side that was so much a part of her that if she dismissed it, I'd be concerned. "King James brought me, if ye dinna recall."

I bared my teeth, losing patience fast. "I recall," I drawled out, hoping she would continue.

"Then why did ye ask? We are to be married."

So much for hope. The chit was a thorn buried deep in my arse. "And why did he leave ye then, when I said nay? I'll need more than your short answers, lass. Mark my words, ye're trying my patience. I'd beat it out of ye if ye were a man."

She smirked, and crossed her arms over her chest, pushing her breasts up, but I avoided staring openly, knowing that was exactly what she wished. "Ye dinna understand your king very well. He gets what he wants. It doesn't matter if ye've said yay

75

or nay, nor does it matter what ye desire. The king's wish is our demand."

"Ah, but ye see..." I circled her, and judging by the way she shifted, I was making her uncomfortable. Good, it was about damn time. I stopped behind her and growled, "I also get what I want."

"Appears not so in this case, though, I canna imagine why ye dinna want to marry me. I'm ten times the woman that simpering whore is."

I gripped her by the arms and whirled her around, my fingers clenching tight to her chin, lifting her face up to mine. "Dinna ever speak about her in such a way. Ye and her could never compare. Never."

"As I said," she retorted haughtily.

I laughed bitterly. "Nay, lass, 'tis as I say, and I'll nay be marrying ye. Not now, nor ever."

Isabella actually had the gall to step toward me this time, "And ye won't be marrying her either."

I had to restrain myself from grabbing hold of her and shaking her so hard her neck snapped. The bite in my voice said no less. "That is not for ye to decide."

She glowered up at me, and through her impudence, her anger, I could see a hint of fear, as though she did dread failing in whatever she'd been tasked with. "Does it matter? The king has deemed it so. He has sworn to never allow ye to marry that whore."

My stomach tightened. I wrenched back my fist, reminding myself that punching a woman went against everything I stood for. Could it be true? Could it be so that he had already expressed such a thing? Not possible. She was bluffing. Playing her cards like the good MacDonald she was. Traitor.

"But ye see, the king has left without a contract written. Ye're at my mercy." I circled her again, stopped behind her, leaned close to her ear and whispered, "Let us pray he doesn't forget ye."

She stiffened. Then turned quickly, our faces only an inch apart. I could see her interest rise, but my disgust did the same. I refused to back down. Refused to step away.

Isabella glanced toward the ground, then coyly back up at me. "My laird, I dinna want either of us to be uncomfortable here."

"Ye mistake me. I'm nay uncomfortable."

She shrugged and walked away, sauntering around the room, not looking at anything in particular which made me think she was stalling. The sudden change was jarring. Unsettling.

"Well, I'll be honest." She whirled. "I am."

To say I was shocked was an understatement. I kept my mouth clamped firmly closed, afraid of how I might comment. I was ready to toss her out the window to be done with her games. Emma didn't play games. She was clear and to the point.

Isabella smiled, though it was rough around the edges. "Ye see, my laird, this is not what I want either. I was perfectly content at my family's seat. Perfectly content to flirt with warriors and dance at feasts and walk the gardens of my mother's home. But now I'm here. Told I must marry a man I know nothing about other than he's a fierce and callous man and everyone seems to hate him."

I narrowed my eyes, not trusting her sudden change in attitude. She walked to the window and stared out—almost longingly. I wasn't buying it.

"I dinna want to be here," she whispered. "I dinna want to marry ye."

"Then why did ye not tell the king?"

A sad smile formed on her thin lips. "'Tis not my choice. My uncle has deemed it so. My mother's brother rules our house. And he petitioned the king who agreed. What am I to do? What am I to say? Nothing. I must comply." She cast me a pitiful look. "Imagine when I arrived to find ye already in love how much further I sank into despair. I'm so sorry for all the pain I've caused Lady Emma. 'Twas not because I have an evil soul, I swear it."

All lies. The devil could take lessons from her. "Ye would have me believe that ye're sincere?" I crossed my arms over my chest and stared at her hard, trying to see into the depths of her dark and cunning eyes.

"Aye. I pray 'tis so."

I scowled, detesting the way she attempted to play me for a fool. "And what would ye have me do?"

She shrugged and her dress slipped slightly off her shoulder. "I suppose ye'll fight every step of the way not to marry me."

I nodded.

"Then spare me the embarrassment of doing so and…"

"And what?"

Her eyes lit up as though she'd just come up with a grand scheme. "Handfast to me," she said in a rush. "We'll not lie together, and after the year ye can send me home on the grounds of never conceiving. Ye'll need an heir. I won't tell."

I shook my head. "There is no plan that leaves ye here for a year that I'll agree to."

"Why?" she pouted.

"Ye're not dense. I'm certain ye can figure that answer out."

"My uncle," she stated with a frown.

"For one."

"Then what do ye suggest?"

"I will reason with the king."

She nodded, looking off into the distance as if contemplating what he said. "Will he be reasoned with?"

I shrugged. Even if Hell froze over I wouldn't discuss my political strategies with this she-devil.

"A drink, then," she said. "Please." Lady Isabella eyed the whisky. "Do not men bond over a drink?"

"I'll not get sotted like your guards."

She laughed, and let the dress slip a little more down her other shoulder as she headed toward the whisky. I did not appreciate her attempts to seduce me.

"I did find that to be rather out of sorts. But I promise I'm not asking for it. Simply a promise over a drink," she said.

"And what promise is that?" I asked, guarded once more.

"That ye won't…dispose of me in a way other than sending me back north."

I frowned, incredulous. "Ye think I'd kill ye to be rid of ye?"

"Have ye not done so to others?" She popped the cork on the whisky.

"I never kill when there is an easier solution."

"Then promise me." She held the decanter of whisky in the air, as if waiting for my agreement to pour.

I nodded. She took two cups aside, and glancing up at me as she poured, I was surprised to see relief in her eyes. Did she truly think I would have her killed?

Isabella stepped around the desk and brought me the cup. I decided in her case fear was a good thing.

"Sláinte," she said.

"Sláinte." I took the cup and downed the contents.

What felt like seconds later I woke with a raging headache, staring up at the ceiling of library. I was on the floor. The cold of the stones chilling my bare arse.

Bare arse…

"What in bloody…" I leaned up on an elbow, the light of the candles burning my eyes.

I was nude from the waist down, shirt tugged up nearly to my armpits, my plaid flung aside like a useless rag. A smear of blood streaked down my cock.

What the bloody hell happened?

Lady Isabella…

The last thing I recalled was her handing me the cup. Of me downing the whisky.

And then waking up like this. There was only one explanation and I was too much a fool to have seen it coming.

She'd drugged me. Same as she had the men. And… *Mo creach*… I stared down at my cock, at my naked abdomen and thighs. The woman couldn't have…

She'd drugged me. Lain with me. If the blood was any indication, I'd deflowered her. Fuck. If I'd not been drugged this would have never happened. Never in a million fucking years. How could I have let down my guard? How did she do it? I watched her pour the whisky for Christ's sake!

I pushed myself up, anger slicing through my veins in painful ribbons of regret. I whirled toward my desk where the flask and cups sat, and with a fit of rage upended it. The desk crashed against the adjacent wall, all its contents hurtling to the floor.

Traitorous bitch! I should have known better than to trust her. Should have refused a drink of truce. Set her on her way. Given her no choice but to leave Gealach. My idiocy caused me to betray the only woman I loved, the light in my forever darkness.

A painful stabbing gored my insides. Nausea from the poison and from what I'd done. I lifted my face toward the ceiling and let out a painful roar. Oh, God. I covered my hands with my face, feeling them shake over my stinging eyes. Emotions I'd never felt bombarded me, overwhelmed me. This couldn't be happening.

I doubled over, unable to help upending the contents of my belly onto the floor.

I couldn't tell Emma. She'd never believe me.

And I didn't even know what happened. I couldn't tell her, because what would I say? I picked up the chair and threw it toward the hearth, watching the wood splinter against the stone.

'Twas time I sought an audience with the king. I'd leave at first light.

CHAPTER EIGHT

Emma

"Over here with that, my lady," Cook called.

The cellar smelled... I couldn't quite describe the scent. Musty wasn't the right word, it wasn't damp, but cool and dry. Maybe earthy was a good word for it. I walked as gingerly as I could toward her, dodging women and men who helped us fill the cellar storeroom. Each of my arms was wrapped around a large sealed jug. We'd been preserving food all morning, an endeavor I'd never imagined before, but with winter coming, it was a task if not completed, the castle inhabitants could very well starve.

Then again... the amount of salt and brine we used in various jugs was giving me a serious case of salt-hate.

I stumbled, jerking forward, but righted myself before I dropped the jars. Cook leapt forward and grabbed one of them from me as I looked down to see what tripped me up. A large piece of cracked pottery. Someone must have dropped it and not cleaned it up. Free from one jug, I picked up the broken piece and put it on an empty shelf—which only made Cook glower at the spot. I'd have to remember to grab it on my way out.

"Careful, lass, wouldn't want to drop the beets now."

"Thank you." And I wouldn't want to. I'd only just discovered how much I liked them. We'd worked hours that morning pickling vegetables, salting fish and meat, hanging herbs and garlic to dry. We'd sliced up what was left of the fruit and preserved them in jars with honey. Baked a thousand oat cakes, and made strips of meat to be dried for jerky, and beans and peas were laid out to dry. Root vegetables and cabbages were all put in baskets with layers of burlap between. My fingers were raw, and my mind blown. All the work we'd done already still wouldn't be enough. Cook said that preserving the food for winter would take a week with all hands on deck—and she had over two dozen clanswomen chipping in to help.

The day's work had to be lugged down to the cellar where it would be stored in the cool room for all of winter. Looking around, everything appeared the same to me. There were no labels, and all the jars were identical. No printed pictures to tell us what was inside.

But I watched as cook tapped her finger along the top shelf until she seemed to find the spot she wanted and then put the pickled beets on top of it. If the woman knew where everything went by counting shelves, than the clan would be in trouble if something happened to her. Without Cook, every meal would be a guessing game.

If Cook thought it odd that I'd never been involved in preparing food for winter, she said nothing. The fact that Logan gave me the title of lady probably helped with that as I was sure there were plenty of ladies who didn't think it their place to do chores. One in particular who stalked the halls of Gealach. God, how I hated her.

Amazing how the presence of one woman could totally destroy my confidence in my position here. There was no doubt in my mind that Logan still loved me, but I knew he, too, struggled with how to deal with the situation, and now it was certain that she was spying, or something along those lines.

"How many more jars of beets?" Cook asked, readjusting the way I'd put my jar up.

"I think five more."

I hoped she'd tell me that was it. I desperately wanted to go back up to my room and tap on the door to see if Logan was next door. I wanted to search the halls until I found him and pull him into a darkened corner.

She nodded. "After that we'll hang the herbs and garlic."

Damn.

A loud thud, followed by the sound of several men cursing, had me whirling to see what they were about. Three men chased a rolling barrel that they must have lost hold of on their way down the stairs.

Cook ran after them, shouting and I stayed back in the shadows, wishing I could melt away. They cleaned up their mess and left the cellar and for the first time I was alone.

I swiped at the hair falling around my face from the bun I'd put it in, sweat soaking it and making loose tendrils stick to my temples. Sitting down on one of the barrels, I rubbed the back of my neck, stretched out my feet. I glanced around at the flickering torches. Only three had been lit, but it was enough to light the shelves we'd been filling, leaving the back of the cellar in shadows. I took several deep breaths, putting myself in that thinking place. The place where I liked to go when I had to figure out some of life's great mysteries.

Before I could reach it, there was a sound from the darkened part of the cellar. A scuffling sound. My gaze shot to the spot, and I squinted, trying to make out what it was. I could only see shadows. Dark and short, wide and thin. The shelves, various boxes and barrels, but my mind made the noise into every imaginable demon.

Another scuffle.

"Hello?"

There was no answer.

Of course.

Then I was reminded of the time I'd snuck down into the darkened secret room fifty feet below the castle. How when I'd reached the bottom, my candles had been blown out. I'd had to crawl in the dark, fear eating me from the inside out until I reached the stairs, and climbed. And climbed. And climbed. And then I'd fallen. Thought I was going over the edge of a cliff, but in reality I'd only tripped and tumbled to the floor.

There had been a ghost or demon or something there with me. Something evil that took away the light. Something dark that wanted me to stay buried.

Was it back?

Goosebumps prickled my skin and I rubbed my arms, standing and backing toward the stairs, suddenly sure that I wasn't alone. I kept my eyes on the darkened shadows, half-expecting a demon to lunge from the dark corners and grab me by the throat.

My foot caught on something and I flailed backward. Strong arms wrapped around my middle and I opened my mouth to scream, but no sound came out. Like I'd been paralyzed and my voice stolen from me.

"Shh..." someone whispered by my ear and a shiver stole over me.

Then a hard, warm body crashed against my back and I sank against it, instantly aware of Logan. A sigh of relief escaped me, and I leaned my head back against his shoulder, his masculine scent surrounding and intoxicating me.

"I am leaving at first light," he said, his voice harsher than his touch.

"To go where?" Panic made my voice sound shrill, and I worked to calm myself.

"I must seek out the king. This is what we both want, is it not?" he asked.

"Yes," I nodded, relieved that he was going to speak with the king so soon, but wondering at his sudden urgency.

"The thing is... I canna take Lady Isabella with me." He frowned and looked off into the shadows, dark thoughts swirling in his eyes. "If I were to bring her, it only gives the king the upper hand to force me into marriage on the spot."

"Then you must leave her here."

Logan's scowl was black and bitter. The interview with her must not have gone well at all. "I dinna want to do that either."

"Do you have another choice?"

His jaw tightened, ticking in a rhythmic pattern. I wanted to reach out, to stroke that erratic muscle and tell him that all would be well, that the king would see the error of his ways, but I had no way of knowing myself, and so the words, so confident in my own ears, couldn't find their way to my lips.

"I will leave my men with strict instructions that the castle is to be on lockdown," he said firmly.

I nodded. "What does lockdown mean?"

"No one leaves. No one comes."

"That's what I figured. How long will you be gone?"

He shook his head. "I know not. The king has gone to Falkland Palace. If the weather cooperates, we could be there in three days, just on his heels. If not, could be as long as a week to reach it."

"A week there and a week back, and how long to speak with the king." Already I was dreading the time he'd be away.

"He will see me right away. I could be there for two days, three at the maximum."

I cringed at his timeline. "So three weeks at the most?"

"Aye, but will likely be less."

He appeared so cold. So hard. There was something wrong, I could feel it in my bones.

"What happened?" I asked softly.

He jerked his gaze back to me, eyes scrutinizing as he searched my face.

"What makes ye think there is something wrong?"

I shrugged. "I can tell. You are..." I looked at him, so stiff and straight, intense and awkward. "You're not yourself." Not even the man I'd first met who was extremely cautious around me. This man was suffering greatly.

"'Tis nothing. I simply must seek out the king and straighten out this farce. We canna have Isabella here. I canna marry her. 'Tis preposterous."

It did not go unnoticed by me that he didn't lament about how he wanted to marry me. That he loved me. I could see his anger, a fury so intense it darkened his eyes to black. The man was possessed by it, and I tried not to take offense at his lack of sentimentality. After all, he was a warrior. I'd known that the moment, I met him. But I'd also seen the softer side. Been inside his heart and heard him declare his love and passion for me. But this man before me now was a man disturbed.

A man on a mission.

A man spurred on by something that greatly troubled him.

What had Isabella done?

Call it woman's intuition, or just gut instinct. "Are you sure that's all?"

He glowered down at me. "I'm positive."

I forced myself to stand where I was, and not to take a step backward. Suddenly all of his intensity was pointing toward me, and my stomach did a little flip.

Logan reached up and grabbed hold of my face with one hand. A thumb on one side of my chin and his fingers on the other. He tugged me forward, his lips crashing on mine in a brutal, forceful kiss.

"Ye're mine," he growled, his teeth pulling at my lower lip. "And I'm yours. Yours alone."

There it was. The declaration I'd been waiting for. I was his and he was mine.

"Yes, mine…" I murmured. "And yours."

Wrapping my arms around him, hands splayed on his lower back, I arched into him. Logan held my face with one hand and roughly gripped my hip with the other. He stroked my flesh, rubbing in circles, roaming over my buttocks and ribs, but never quite touching the parts that ached to be caressed. Teasing, taunting, always.

Logan liked to see me strung up tight. To feel me quiver with wanting, and to witness the way my body responded, wet and coiled. And I liked to show him how much I wanted him.

Cock pressed tight to the juncture of my thighs he walked me backward into the shadows. I clutched to him. Mouth a tangle of frenzied licks and sucks. Hands stroking over his flesh, and his burning a path over mine. Minutes before I'd been running from the shadows, not wanting to discover what was within them. But now, with Logan pushing me past my fears, I eagerly retreated. Willingly, I walked without being able to see what was behind me, only in front. And before me was a powerful, sensual, wicked man. I wanted nothing more than to feel his hot rod of pleasure as it drove inside me.

Pressing me up against the wall, Logan dragged in a breath. "God, lass, ye drive me to the brink." He skimmed his lips over my chin, burning a sizzling path, until he reached my ear. I was shaking with need as he spoke. "I've never wanted someone more in my life than I want ye. I've never needed someone as much as I need ye. I've never felt—"

But he cut himself off. The deep turmoil circulating in each word as it was expressed chilled me. He sounded vulnerable.

Hurt. Aching. Tortured. The man was struggling inside, and even if he didn't want to tell me what it was, I knew how to comfort him. Together we were powerful. Together we were freed from the demons that tormented us.

I slipped my hands into the waist of his belted kilt, running them around the back toward the front until I reached the warmed metal of the buckle.

"I love you, Logan," I said, my lips pressed to the crook of his shoulder. I unhooked the belt, ran my hands up over his chest and plucked at the pin that held the layer of his plaid thrown over his shoulder, then listened as the fabric unraveled, falling with a muffled thud on the floor. "Together we'll get through this."

Again he drew in a ragged breath, compelling me to implore him once more to tell me what weighed heavy on his heart. But before I could utter the words, his lips captured mine and he pressed his naked hips against me. The heat of his flesh seared a path through my clothes and I was suddenly desperate to be out of them.

I'd noticed more and more often that our lovemaking wasn't so much about lessons, about the struggle for power and acceptance, but more about connection. About joining together and sharing. About being one.

Maybe that was the lesson. How to give in to each other.

Logan tugged at my gown, his fingers sliding easily through the ties, loosening it until he could ease it over my shoulders, down my arms and leave it slack at my waist. His warm palm covered my breast, only the thin chemise I wore separating us now. My nipple was already puckered from anticipation, but now it fairly bulged with the need to feel him stroke it with his tongue.

And then he was wrenching it away, the delicate fabric shredding with his determination.

I reached a leg around his, hooking it behind his knee, trying as I might to get his cock closer to my clit, where I loved to feel his hardness stroke.

I moaned. "I want you so bad."

"Ye have no idea."

"Will anyone come down?"

"Nay, I told Cook I needed to speak with ye privately."

"But—"

"Shh... If they come, then they can watch. They can see me lick your quim."

And with that, he dropped to his knees and cold air wafted over my ankles and calves as he lifted my gown over his head and disappeared.

I pressed my back to the wall, hands digging into the plaster as his hot mouth hovered over my wet and quivering sex. My netherlips pulsed, clit twinged, every nerve-ending on fire with excitement.

I dug my hands into his hair as he parted my folds with his fingers and then put his tongue on me. A long, heady, slow stroke from the opening of my sex to the very top, where he swirled around my clit as though I were a melting ice cream cone.

"Oh, God," I gasped.

"Uh-uh," I heard him murmur, the sound of his voice vibrating deliciously against my over-sensitized flesh. "Oh, Logan."

I spread my thighs wider and canted my hips forward. "Oh, Logan," I murmured.

"Aye, lass, oh me."

He tantalized me with that tongue, making me breathless, hot and sweaty. I could barely hold up my weight on my legs, and thanked heaven for the strength of the wall behind me.

Torrents of pleasure rocked me. He drew on my clit, sucking, making it pulse and then scraped his teeth over it before flattening his tongue and stroking in quick short bursts before sucking again. It was a new pattern, designed to torment me. To bring me close to the edge, and draw it out.

"Dinna finish, lass, dinna dare."

My breath hitched and I held it, squeezing my eyes shut and forcing myself not to come when every second I was closer and closer to bursting. Suck, scrape, stroke. Suck, scrape, stroke. I moaned, whimpered, gasped, never truly drawing in a breath.

"Now, baby, now," he murmured, stroking fast with the flat of his tongue and thrusting his fingers inside me, pumping hard.

There was no question, I was there, ready for it and I sparked, firing off an orgasm that was so strong I lurched forward, unable to control the convulsions of my body. He continued his tormenting licks until every last wave subsided, and then he stood, whipped me around and yanked up the back of my gown. I gasped. My bare nipples scraped against the rough wall as he pushed me against it, growling with that feral, masculine sound that made my sex quiver anew.

He slapped me hard on the ass and I groaned, hips automatically bucking backward, between my thighs dripping and clenching, waiting.

I felt him drag his cock through the crack of my ass. He pressed the tip to the opening of my sex and I tried to press back, to feel him slide inside me, but he pulled back an inch, uttering, "Not yet."

Biting my lip, I waited on bated breath for what was to come. Suddenly my back was cold as he moved away from me, but I couldn't move, felt glued to the plastered wall, its harsh surface scraping my sensitive flesh. He dragged something closer. What was it?

And then his hand was stroking up my thigh, his fingers pressing deep into the tissue.

"Put your leg up," he demanded, his fingers curling beneath my knee.

I lifted my foot, putting it on top of the barrel he'd pulled near us. He stepped behind me again, fingers tickling over my clit and I groaned.

"Ye're so damn wet." Logan pressed his thick, hard cock against me again. "Do ye know how fucking delicious that is?"

I whimpered, unable to say anything intelligible, as all I could think about was him pounding hard into me from behind.

He grabbed hold of my hip with one hand and pulled me back as he guided the tip of his shaft to my opening.

"Please," I begged.

Lips pressed to my ear he said, "Ye want me to fuck ye?"

"Yes."

"Hard?"

"Yes."

"Put me inside ye."

I reached between my thighs, barely able to grip his cock in my hand, and I guided it toward me, pressing the tip inside, feeling the rim of my sex stretch to accommodate him. My eyes rolled back as I moaned, pushed back with my hips and feeling his cock slide from my fingers and inside my body.

"Fuck me," he demanded.

Hands pressed to the wall, I pushed back, canted my pelvis forward. He stood still behind me, his hands on my hips, teeth scraping my neck.

"Fuck me hard, Emma," he growled.

I eagerly obliged, rocking back and forth with fury, my body squeezing tight to him.

"I want ye to feel my cock going in and out of ye."

"How?" I managed to utter between moans.

"Touch yourself. Rub yourself and as ye do it, slid your fingers lower, slipping them around my cock. Feel me move within ye."

Eliza Knight

I lowered my hand back to my clit, unable to help circling it, stroking it, then lower, until I felt his cock moving in and out of me, slippery and velvet hard. Spreading my fingers wide, I pushed back, his cock sliding in and out from between my pointer and middle finger as he fucked me and I touched myself.

It was more than I could handle, and I cried out as an orgasm tore through me unexpectedly.

"Naughty, Emma," he murmured, biting my earlobe, and slapping my ass.

I shuddered, and even though I'd just come, I felt my body begin to stir again, readying itself for more pleasure.

He kissed me on my back, his tongue drawing circles over one shoulder blade and then another.

"Do ye want to come again?" he asked.

I nodded, then realized he probably couldn't see me in the dark. "Yes."

"Make yourself come again." He tapped lightly over my ribs until he reached the side of my breast and then he cupped it, pinching my nipple. "I want to feel you come on my tongue."

He dropped behind me, pressed his face to my backside, his tongue thrusting inside my cunt, his hands gripping hard to my ass.

I was beyond reason. Beyond everything except immense pleasure. I stroked myself harder, my fingers making circles around and around my clit, up and down, sliding back to feel his tongue inside me, then back to my clit, and then he slicked his tongue upward, rimming around the star between my ass cheeks and I jerked forward, the sensation all together euphoric and so wickedly, forbidden. Oh, I was a naughty girl. And I liked it. Liked it too much, and suddenly as he was licking my ass, I was fingering myself frantically, pushing in and out and then sliding up to rub my clit. Sensing my desperate need, Logan replaced my fingers with his own, plunging them deep

93

as he continued to stroke his tongue over that forbidden part of me, leaving me to rub my clit in glorious panicked swirls.

This time when I came, a scream tore from my throat and I convulsed violently, legs buckling. Logan caught me, holding me where he wanted me, and then he was thrusting inside me. Not waiting for me to recover, but his cock tormenting me all the more. I was on fire, like lava, melting and completely destroyed.

He fucked me hard, fast and I could barely hold against the wall as he rode me, and he, too, was crying out, plunging deeper as he orgasmed.

Neither of us moved, both so consumed by the power of our sex. By the sheer intensity of it.

And then he spoke, his voice hoarse. "I'm going to miss ye."

I shivered, feeling a deep-seated fear at his words. Come the morning, he would be gone.

CHAPTER NINE

Emma

I slept like the dead.

I woke, startled by sounds coming from outside, forgetting momentarily where I was—and what era. I was disoriented, light-headed. I glanced to the right, finding Logan's side of the bed empty. Where had he gone? Judging from the small amount of light coming from the window, it couldn't be much past dawn.

I managed to climb from bed, feet hitting the icy ground. I shivered, rubbing my arms to keep warm and stumbled toward the window. I stubbed my toe on a chair and let out a string of curses in Gaelic that I'd heard Logan mutter when he'd done the same thing. We really ought to move the damn thing, or else our toes would be mangled by the end of year.

That brought a smile to my face and the memories of the past months full force to mind. I'd never been happier.

And then, just like that, my smile faded, replaced by a sour feeling in my belly, and a dryness to my tongue. Logan was leaving today. For as long as three weeks.

An eternity.

I groaned and peeled back the fur covering the window, feeling the draft through the wooden slats. I opened the wooden shutter, shivering at the chill and gazed down at the courtyard.

Men ran to and fro, piling bags on horses, and women stuffed the bags full of supplies. Warriors stood in the center, armed to the teeth and awaiting their laird.

Would he leave without saying goodbye? A cursory glance around the courtyard did not show him to be present. I scurried back to the bed and pressed my hand to the rumpled sheets where he'd lain. Cold.

He'd been gone awhile. Knowing Logan, he probably barely slept.

With the castle in this much of an uproar, he was bound to be leaving within the hour. The very thought sent a shiver of dread through me. My already frozen limbs, fingers and toes dropped another ten degrees, as if my blood refused to flow when we were parted. I hurried to my wardrobe, pulling out a gown, my cloak and boots, and then struggled into them.

Going on six months wasn't nearly enough time to become acquainted with the clothing. I feared I might always need a little help in the dressing department. Knowing what was coming, if I ever had to go to court where the king presided, I'd be sewn into my clothes. Stiff, thick fabrics encrusted with jewels. I crinkled my nose, feeling uncomfortable already. Being at the castle, working side by side with the people, cuddling up with Logan, those things came easy. But court? A royal court with all those pompous people? I shook my head. That, I was not ready for.

I bent over, tugging the last boot over my heel when the door between our rooms slid open and Logan stepped through.

I looked up at him, forgetting all about the laces on my boot and ran toward him. He held out his arms, catching me against his solid form. His clothes were cold, but the warmth of his body seeped through. He smelled crisp and cool like the outdoors, mixed with his own spicy scent.

"I wish you didn't have to go," I said.

"I know it, love. If only we could turn back the clock. I'd have insisted on the king taking Isabella with him. Or even sent a missive telling him not to come."

I shook my head and looked up at him, studying every line and plane on his rugged and devilishly handsome face. "I'm not sure that would have done any good. The king had it in his mind to come here, and who he'd bring. What could you have done? You wouldn't have run from him, or abandoned your people."

Logan glanced down at me, stroking his thumb across my cheek. "Nay, lass, but I would have married ye the moment ye agreed to be my lover."

I buried my face in his chest, gripping tight to his linen shirt and breathing in his scent, burning it in my memory.

"I've put you in danger," I said. "The king..."

"Shh." He stroked his hands on my back, comforting me in the cocoon of his embrace. "The king will not harm me."

"I know but—"

He gripped my shoulders and pulled me back as he bent toward me, so we were face to face. "Do ye recall what ye said yesterday in the storeroom?"

Ummm... yes. And none of it had anything to do with him leaving. I felt the heat rise in my cheeks.

"Not that, lass," he laughed. "Ye said that together we would get through this, and ye were right. Trust me. Trust us."

"I do." I chewed on my lower lip, glancing down at the way his shirt opened, revealing just a splash of tan, muscled chest. "But, Logan, I'm not an idiot. The king will do whatever he wants and from what you've said he can be a vindictive man. What if he takes offense to what you want? What if he demands you stay there and he comes to fetch Isabella? What if he decides he's had enough of his secret brother and...and..." I couldn't even bring myself to say the words.

Logan frowned, the muscle in his jaw ticking. When he spoke, his voice was deadly calm and serious. "I swear by all that is holy that I will not marry that woman. Ye are the only one for me. No matter what she says, what she does, or what the king decries, she will *not* be my wife."

By the end of his little tirade, his teeth were bared and he looked off into the distance as if contemplating some deadly obstacle.

I was getting him riled up and angry. Not the way I wanted to part with him. I wanted our last moments together, before three torturous weeks began, to be pleasant and memorable.

"I'm going to miss you." I wrapped my arms around his middle and laid my head on his chest. "The bed will be so cold without you to curl up against."

He chuckled, his chest rumbling against my ear. "Is that all ye think I'm good for? Warming your toes?"

I giggled. "And my hands."

Logan stroked a heavy hand up and down my back, curled his finger around a tendril of my hair. "The time will fly. I promise. Just think about what's to come. And if anything..." He trailed off as though he, too, didn't want to travel down that path again.

"Tell me. We should leave no questions unanswered."

"If ye find yourself to be in danger, for any reason, hide in the secret chamber."

"*The* secret chamber?" I shuddered. I'd not been back to that dank, decrepit place since Logan showed me the doors. The doors that could lead to death or life.

"Aye. That chamber. No one will find ye there, unless they know of the door, and even then... There are places to hide."

I smirked. "Yeah, and I might never come out again."

"I need to give ye something."

He pulled away and reached into his left boot, pulling out the special dirk he'd shown me before, with the hilt carved from a deer's antler. Twisting it open, Logan once more revealed the iron key to the doors in the secret chamber.

"This key is verra important. It means everything to me."

I shook my head and took a step back. "Then please don't give it to me. I can't be in charge of it. What if I lose it?"

"Ye won't lose it." Logan said it like it was a statement, a fact. So confident was he that I'd not dare lose it. "'Tis important, Emma, that ye listen to me verra carefully."

He gazed intently into my eyes, making the pit of my stomach churn.

"Guard this with your life. Whoever has the key is the Guardian of Gealach."

I shook my head violently. "No, no, no. I don't want it. I can't." There was no way on God's green earth, or hell's high water that I was going to take on the role he requested of me. "I just can't, Logan. I'm not strong like you. I don't know how to take care of people. Before I came here I could barely take care of myself. You can't do this. I can't do this."

Panic made me tremble and my stomach suddenly felt like it was on fire. Another step had me wobbling as my boot lace caught under my foot.

"Emma—"

"What is it you fear will happen while you're gone? What has possessed you to give me this key? This duty?" I hated that my voice shook, that I was suddenly so weak in front of him.

"Emma, love." He pulled me in roughly, kissed me on the forehead and then held me at arm's length again. "Ye can do this. 'Tis not that I fear something will happen to me. I have every intention of returning to you, and as swiftly as I can. But this key"—he held it up in front of my eyes—"is the key to the castle. The key to everything. Ye know how much MacDonald wants to get his hands on it."

"Precisely why you should have it." I raised my hands a little. Exasperated. "I mean, you are much stronger than me. I'm going to be here alone with that hellish woman. She could take it from me."

"Ye won't let her."

"How can you be sure? My room has been broken into before. What's to say it's not broken into again? Maybe she'll decide to ransack it the moment you leave."

"Ye will keep the key on ye. Just as I have kept it on me. Never leave the room without it. Let the key burn its place against ye, so that ye may never be without it."

I shook my head again, fearing more the great responsibility of holding the key, rather than any harm that could come to me from holding it. "What if it falls out of my boot?"

Logan looked at me seriously, his brows drawn together in concentration. "Ye will strap it to your thigh."

"My thigh?" This was the stuff of westerns when saloon dollies and gun-slinging women holstered pistols to their thighs amidst their garters. That wasn't me.

"Aye, sit."

But, maybe, I had to become that woman if I was going to survive here.

Logan led me over to the chair, nudging me to sit in it. He knelt before me and took my foot up onto his bent knee. With slow, measured movements he slid the skirt of my gown and chemise up over my thigh, revealing my flesh to his gaze. I was suddenly hot. Overcome with need, and his face was only a foot away from my sex, which was nearly drenched. I was certain he could sense my desire, smell it as he breathed deep.

He grinned at me, wicked intent in his eyes. "Wish that I did not have to leave. I'd fuck ye in this chair."

My breath caught and I nodded. "I'd like that."

Logan cleared his throat and stood, walking over to the wardrobe and rummaging through it and then disappearing through our joined doorway into his own chamber. He quickly returned with a leather strap and I was swiftly reminded of how he'd tied me to his bed and made love to me, and also of how much I wanted him to do that again. To feel the leather around my wrists and know I couldn't touch him, that I had to surrender to him. I squirmed in the chair, parted my legs so that when he knelt before me again he could see the folds of my sex glistening.

One of the best medieval ideals—no underwear. Forget thongs and sheer, lacy panties. Here, I wore nothing and it was hotter than hell. When I could feel myself getting wet, the heat of it slick and sexy against my thighs, it made me all the hotter.

Logan licked his lips, staring now at the view I'd given him. "Ye're a tease, lass."

"I'm only showing you how much I want you." I flicked my gaze toward his belt. "Want to show me how much you want me?"

He groaned.

I leaned forward, loving when he let me play the seductress. I reached my hand down and grabbed hold of his thick cock through the fabric of his plaid.

God, I wanted him.

"Just once before you leave," I begged. "It won't take long." I patted the arm of the chair. "We can do it right here."

Logan stood so abruptly I nearly upended the chair. He pulled me up and turned, sitting where I'd been. He flipped his kilt out of the way, revealing his length in all its vibrant glory. Long, hard, a vein traveling up the middle to meet at the tip of his engorged head. A drop of pre-cum glistened the tip. "Lift your gown."

I lifted up the gown around my hips and stepped forward. He scooted to the edge of the chair and then grabbed hold of my hips, effortlessly lifting me until I straddled him. He held me aloft a minute, allowing me to grab hold of his thick shaft and position him at my opening, and then he yanked me down, thrusting his hips upward at the same time.

Both our heads fell back as we moaned, that initial joining, the thrust and sink, so hot and pleasurable that there is nothing one can do but surrender to it.

This would be no lengthy coupling, but quick and furious. He gripped tight to my ass, thrusting up, fast and hard as I rocked back and forth, my hands finding anchor against his shoulders. I sank closer, kissing his lips, nuzzling his neck, and he teased over the flesh of my nipples with his teeth, sucking on them and leaving wet spots on my gown from his tongue.

I cried out, my body tensing with each ensuing push and pull. I was so wound up. Emotions, fear, tension, all of it pushing us both closer to the brink.

Logan buried his face between my breasts, murmuring words filled with passion, emotion and something deeper — regret? I pushed it aside, unwilling to explore what that could mean. Instead, I whispered my own words of love, of sensuality. Telling him how much I liked his cock thrusting hard and deep inside me. How much I loved him, needed him.

When the fluttering of my orgasm began, I cried out, "I'm coming," and he ground his hips upward harder, faster, until seconds later we were both crying out and quaking with mutual release.

"I dinna want to leave ye, but I have to go," he said, his voice gravelly against my breasts.

I stroked my hand through his hair, tugged until he looked up at me. I bent low and met my lips to his. "I know. But ye'll be back soon, we both know it. We must both do what has to be done."

I climbed from atop him and lifted my foot right between his thighs, my toes an inch from his balls and his cock still partially erect and glistening from our sex. "Strap it on me," I demanded with a coy smile.

Logan grinned and leaned forward, pressing his lips to my knee. "What would I do without ye, Emma? Ye make me stronger. Just when I thought nothing could give me more power, here ye are."

He grabbed the leather strap from the table and wrapped it around my thigh. "Tight but not too tight," he instructed. He Wrapped it around twice, leaving the second tying even looser. "Watch as I do this, I want to see ye do it after me."

Logan picked up the dirk and slipped it between my thigh and the second loop, sheathed blade facing downward. Then he twisted the blade up and around that same strap, making a tight loop of its own. Once more he flipped the blade up and tucked it back down, this time into the initial loop he'd made around my thigh.

"Triple looped," he said with a smile and tug. "'Twill not go anywhere. Give it a yank."

I tugged at the weapon, and it did feel secure.

"Now ye try it."

I untied the leather and rewrapped it, following his lead of triple securing the blade. The first time it was too loose. The second time too tight, but by the third go, I had it done just as perfectly as Logan.

"Good. Ye're ready."

"I don't know if I'm ready," I said, "but I will keep your dagger hidden."

His eyes darkened and he gazed at me seriously. "Dinna let anyone see the dirk. Dinna let anyone touch it, have it."

"What about Agatha?" I asked, the woman dressed me, how was she not to see it?

Logan shook his head. "Even Agatha. No one is to know. When she comes to dress ye, slip it beneath the mattress. When she finishes, tie it on. Wear it at all times, even when ye sleep."

"And what about when I'm in the bath?"

"Slip it under the mattress again."

I was still scared. Could feel the fear skittering up and down my spine. This was a huge task he was giving me. The key to the castle, to all his secrets. "I'll guard it with my life."

"I'd rather ye simply guard it with your thigh." He smiled. "I dinna want ye to give your life for it. And for that matter, I rather like your thighs." He gazed down at the dirk strapped to the front of my leg. "Damn, but that's sexy, lass."

I smiled and kissed him again. But then I grew serious once more. "What if someone does discover it? Say I'm attacked and they see it on my leg?"

"Ye won't be attacked."

I rolled my eyes. "I know, I'll be safe, got it, but what *if*?"

"Dinna let anyone have that knife, Emma. I'd rather see it burned in a fire, melted to nothing and never be able to get behind those doors than see it get into the wrong hands."

I swallowed. "All right."

"Ye will be safe."

"Why do I get the feeling your convincing yourself more than me?" I asked.

He gave a short, quiet laugh. "'Haps I am."

"How many of your men will you take with you?"

"Just a dozen. I'm leaving the rest, ready for war."

"Is it that serious?"

He nodded. "With me gone, our enemies are very likely to descend upon this place. But ye will be safe. My men have safeguarded Gealach for over a decade. No one has ever defeated us."

"No one has ever defeated *you*."

He smiled up at me, a sad edge to the curve of his lips. "There have been times when I've not been present, and Ewan has always defeated the enemy. I have every confidence he will continue to impress me."

"Ewan is remaining behind?" Just the knowledge of that made me feel better.

"Aye, lass. He'll take care that no harm comes to ye."

"And Lady Isabella? What will she be doing?"

He glowered again, any humor in him instantly gone with the mention of her name. "No doubt getting into trouble." He looked up at me, worry crinkling his eyes. "Dinna believe anything that bitch says, Emma."

His words were spoken fiercely, so much hatred in them I took a step back.

"I won't," I whispered.

"She's hell in female form," he ground out, standing up. "Drugged two of my guards, possibly more..." He trailed off, and I had the sudden sinking sensation that there was something he wasn't telling me. Something important.

"I would have avoided her at all costs without your warning," I murmured. I'd had enough dealings with her to last me a lifetime and I wouldn't be unhappy to see her go.

Logan gave a curt nod, and pulled me into his arms. "I've tarried long enough now that my men may begin to search for me. I'd not want them to think I'd come up here for a last minute bit of warming before I leave when I'd forbidden them to do so."

"Why would you forbid them?" I asked, looking up into his darkly handsome face.

"A man who yearns for home, comes home."

"Will you not yearn for it?" I asked.

"Desperately so."

CHAPTER TEN

Logan

*E*very man paused before urging his horse through the gates of Gealach and onto the waiting moor. Leaving the safety of the stone fortress was a concern, but I thought more, each man feared what we'd find upon our return.

To stand a moment in prayer for safety beneath the gate was custom, and a tradition not one man would forget.

I trusted Ewan explicitly. But, I thought, as I turned back, the arching gate over my head, taking in the towering turrets, the wall walk and the window to Emma's chamber, catching a glimpse of her fiery hair, there was more to worry over than what would happen while we were away. Would Emma be there when I returned? Or would the miracle of time-travel have sucked her back to whatever life she'd led before me?

Would Isabella harm her? Torture Emma with how she'd drugged me, used me? No doubt, she'd make it into something well beyond what it was. God, I should have said something to Emma. I completely ignored Isabella before leaving. Didn't want to speak with her and have her taunt me, but I also hoped by ignoring her, she'd feel that her plan didn't work. By all means I should have come barreling in on her, and I did not.

A gentle breeze beckoned me. Calming in its caress. How many demons now waited in the trees beyond the moors, watching as we departed?

It was almost enough to make me turn back. But then I recalled what had occurred—or rather what I didn't know transpired—in my library. The blood on my cock. The drugs in my whisky. A flash of memory I'd not recalled before jarred me. Isabella's triumphant grin as she nudged my shoulders. I was on the ground and she grabbed onto my belt. She said something, but I couldn't hear it, only saw the movement of her lips. And then it was gone in a whisper of smoke.

Bloody fucking hell!

Anger shredded my insides and I bared my teeth, turning back to the road ahead. I'd been defeated within my own walls by a conniving bitch and I couldn't let her get away with it. I had to give my demands to the king and make him see reason. And I prayed hard that my mind would recall every minute or at least enough of it that I could piece together what had happened. Even knowing what happened, wouldn't relieve me of the tremendous guilt of having betrayed Emma.

I'd told her that she was to be mine and that I'd not love another, not touch another. Isabella had taken away that choice. There was only one other person who'd ever been able to take away my choice and it was my brother, the bloody king. I'd promised myself long ago that there would be no one else to decide my fate for me. And I meant it.

If worse came to worse, I would take fate into my own hands and see that Isabella disappeared forever.

When I returned from seeking the king's audience, I would tell Emma everything. Pray that she still accepted me. It was too great a secret to keep from her. But telling her before I had spoken to the king wouldn't have helped anything.

I had to leave her behind in order to grasp onto her forever. Had to trust that the four foot thick walls of the castle and my men could protect her. Had to trust the safety of Gealach and its inhabitants to Ewan's very capable hands.

Had to trust that she wouldn't believe a word of Isabella's vile tongue.

I couldn't be worried over it. Had to relinquish that bit of power in order to seize control over the rest of my life.

As the last of my dozen men exited the gate, the lot of us dressed in hunting plaids in order to disguise ourselves from enemies. I called out our progressions. "Forward!"

The men grunted their reply in unison. Lined two by two, we spurred our horses into gallops, setting the pace for the grueling trip toward the king. I spurred my mount further, leaning over his withers, not caring that his hair slapped painfully against my cheeks. 'Twas nowhere near the punishment I deserved.

Baring my teeth I growled at the wind. Come hell or high water, we'd make it to the king's court in record time.

Breaking through the trees, heading southward, we followed the well beaten road, lighted more now that the massive, ancient trees had lost their leaves, and only their gnarled claw-like branches scratched the sky. Many thought these woods to be haunted. The trees to be alive and fae and other tricky creatures to live within the hidden coves and hollowed out oaks. But I'd always found comfort in the forest. Loving the way its natural foliage wrapped around me, cocooning me in a shroud of mystery. There was always a place to hide, always nourishment to be found. Nay, this place was not haunted, but blessed.

Ahead, I spied a large tree that had fallen in the road. I frowned. If the tree had truly fallen, my scouts would have seen it removed. This tree was laid their purposefully. I raised a hand, halting my men, instantly on alert.

'Twas an ambush, I was sure of it.

We scanned the trees, looking for anything out of the ordinary.

I pointed toward a spot not twenty feet beyond the fallen tree. A body, on the ground. Unmoving. Wearing our colors.

Damn. I gritted my teeth. Red hair matted his face. Looked like one of the twins, my best scouts. I signaled to my men to stay behind as I went forward to investigate for myself. The closer I got, the more it became apparent that it was indeed Collum, one of the twins. He laid motionless, blood seeping from a jagged wound in his throat. He'd been murdered, viciously. His clothes were torn and bloody from multiple slash wounds. Weapons were gone, leaving him to look vulnerable even in the afterlife.

Where was his brother?

I scrutinized our surroundings, certain to find his body next. And I did. Just a hint of discoloration on the forest floor where Tavish's red hair splayed on top of dead leaves. I turned back to my men and nodded toward the forest and two of them broke off. This close to the castle, we'd not bury them here, but bring them back to their family. I had to harden my heart, when what I truly wanted to do was sink to the ground, my knees touching dirt and shout up to the sky. Why did Collum and Tavish have to suffer? Why did they have to serve as some sort of warning to us? These men were good to us. Loyal. Genius in their abilities to scout, and now they lay dead in service to me, cut down by my enemies.

But there wasn't time for me to mourn. Instead of falling to my knees in prayer, I gritted my teeth and scrutinized our surroundings. There was no sight of anyone ready to ambush us. No shifting shadows amongst the barren trees, no whispers on the breeze. Nothing beyond the shifting of our horses' feet, their puffs of breath, the jangling of the reins and stretching sounds of our leather saddles. But I knew in my gut, this was not simply a warning, a blow to where they thought it would hurt.

Our enemies knew better than to let us simply walk away. They wanted to rattle us. To put us in a state of mind where all rationality disappeared.

I couldn't allow that to happen.

I locked eyes with each of my men and nodded. "Hold steady," I said. Two simple words they were, but for the men it was a great boost. Their leader was holding steady, and so should they.

The moments ticked by in a torrent of heartbeats. I focused on slowing mine, on defeating these men for all they stood for and for what they stood in the way of. They needed to be removed so we could be about our business to the king.

Then I heard it. A whistle on the wind. I ducked and an arrow went whizzing over my back, stabbing into the tree not a foot away. I rent the air with a fierce battle cry.

The sounds of metal scraping on scabbards as swords were wrenched free, pierced the air as my men's answering call.

"Formation!" I cried, and the men were quick to move, all of us putting our horses' rears together in a circle in order to protect each other's backs.

They swung at us from trees, flying past like animals as they tried to slice at us from the sky before landing on foot. And though they may have thought their tactics were clever, they were no match for our men on horses.

A crude looking bunch they were, dirty, scuffed and covered in muck. They looked like the devil's minions crawling the earth. They sprang at us, despite their disadvantage, lunging forward and stabbing at the horses' chests. But we kept our horses plated, and each stab did nothing but irritate the mounts all the more.

My own horse, reared, pawing the air and planting a blow against one rat's chest. He flew backward with the force of the jolt, crying out with his hands clutched to his chest. He'd likely find it hard to breathe.

The next who leapt forward, saw the end of my sword sink into his shoulder, before I wrenched up, tearing his arm from his body. He stumbled away, pale and in shock as he lay dying on the ground.

A few more swung in from the skies on ropes tied high in the trees, but this time we knew the way of their descent and each one of them was cut down before he had a chance to act.

The next group to rush us did so from the ground, leaping up and striking out. A few got in a scrape or two, but they were at once put down like the rabid dogs they were.

"Where is MacDonald?" I bellowed. "Show yourself, ye coward!"

But only the rustle of leaves answered me. The man did not appear, and no one else attacked us. We waited for several moments before dismounting and making piles of the dead for a quick burial.

Though they were our enemies, they did not deserve to rot in the open without a chance to explain their evil deeds to the Lord on high.

"My laird." I turned at the sound of Gregor's voice. "This one's still with us."

I marched forward, pointing my sword tip into a gaping wound on his belly. "Tell me where MacDonald is, and we may yet let ye live."

The man cringed, clutching at a lesser wound on his arm, and gasping for breath.

"Tell me," I demanded, digging into the wound.

He screamed, his lips turning into nearly the same milky-white of his face.

"He's... he's..." But he didn't finish, instead, sobbed and gagged.

"I will have my men take ye back to the castle. We have a healer who can sew up these wounds. All ye have to do is tell us where he is."

Hope lit his already dulling eyes. "I..." He gasped and cringed. "I... He's not here."

"Where is he?"

"We were to wait for him."

"How long?"

"Within a fortnight he said he'd be here to claim Gealach." The man sucked in a deep breath and then spat at me. "To claim *his* place."

I wiped the spittle from the front of my jerkin. "Before ye muttered all that nonsense, I'd been in a forgiving mood." I shoved my blade the rest of the way into his wound and twisted. "Now, I'm not so forgiving."

The man screamed, and then was suddenly silent as his life left him.

The ruffians lay dead all around us. Thank God, and our skill with the blade, for it. These men would have, without a doubt, tried to attack the castle. Isabella could have tricked or drugged my men by now and opened the door when they arrived. Hopefully the men would have the foresight to guard their drinks as I'd warned.

I glanced at Gregor. Sweat glistened his face and his eyes were crinkled with fury, mirroring my own image I was sure. "I'm sorry for the loss of your men," I said. "Collum and Tavish will not be forgotten. I need ye to take them and a message back to the castle. Warn the men, and Ewan, that MacDonald will attack soon and to be ready. Dinna mention a fortnight. The man could be lying. I wouldn't be surprised is the traitor bastard was headed to the gate now, or already there."

My gaze flicked painfully toward the road to Gealach. I gritted my teeth against the intense need to return. I couldn't. Not yet.

"Tell Ewan to lock Isabella in her room. She canna be trusted." I nodded, as if just now accepting this truth myself. I should have locked her up before I left. Regretted not having done it. "MacDonald is an enemy of the crown, he is to be treated as such. Tell Ewan to gather more scouts. The clansmen are to hole up as if a siege is upon us. I dinna want to lose one more."

CHAPTER ELEVEN

Emma

*T*he wind blew in frigid bursts on top of the battlements overlooking Gealach's lands. I'd been standing there for at least two hours. Looking out over the gently swaying marshy grasses, the eerily tranquil waters of the loch and the intimidating starkness of the forest. I don't know what I was waiting for, or why. But the intensity of my need was such that even the numbness of my fingers and painful sting of cold swirling up the skirts of my gown couldn't make me leave my post.

Logically, I knew I couldn't stand here for the weeks it took until Logan returned. But, even with that knowledge present, I couldn't pull away. Had to stand here. Had to wait. Had to ride out the fear that rode shotgun in my heart.

Felt the deep necessity to stand guard. Not that I'd be able to do anything, should I see something amiss. I had no weapons. I had no way of shouting out to anyone, for my voice would not be carried on the wind. I was also not an authority figure, despite the dagger that burned a hole in my thigh.

I'd be lying if I said I wasn't scared shitless. Logan had only ever left the castle before for a few hours at a time—scouting, hunting or working on his ships. When he was gone, I stayed in my room or helped out Cook, fearing the unknown and whether or not he'd return. Two or three weeks was completely different and I was almost certain I wouldn't spend any time in my own chamber. No, I'd be in his. I'd lock both our doors, opening up the sliding wood panel between our chambers and curl into Logan's bed, feeling safe in the large stark bed—though it mirrored mine.

I'd confiscated one of his linen shirts, too, his scent still captured in the woven fabric. I'd probably be sleeping in that every night.

A rider break through the forest trees traveling at a speed that would likely kill a lesser animal.

"Oh my God."

I leaned forward, heedless to the frozen stone on my fingertips as I watched. His beast was massive, strong, and resembled the stock Logan kept in his stables. The colors of his plaid matched that of the warriors who'd left over a couple hours before. My heart lodged in my throat.

"No," I whispered, leaning further still over the side and blinking furiously, willing the vision away.

My heart skipped a beat, launching itself up into my throat and choking me. Unable to breathe, unable to steady myself, I looked frantically from side to side. There was no one up here with me. The men were posted at their respected stations—away from me, precisely the reason I'd chosen this quiet spot.

Had they seen the rider? Did they know something was going on?

I prayed they did, tried to listen to see if I could hear shouting, but I all I was aware of was the pounding of my heart and the way the wind had shifted and picked up speed.

"Rider!" I called, certain no one would hear me.

The riding warrior raised his arm in the air and waved it. Was there an answering call? A wave? I leaned over the stone, trying to catch a view of the courtyard and the gate tower. Dammit! I could hardly see anything with my hair whipping into my face.

And I heard nothing, besides the wind.

Shoving away from the stone, I ran to the wooden door that led to the narrow stairwell. I had to get to the courtyard, had to find out what was happening. I tugged at the door, but it wouldn't budge. Oh, my God, had someone locked me up here? Anticipated me freezing to death?

I wrapped both hands around the iron. Twisted, yanked, nearly pulled my shoulders from the sockets. This couldn't be happening. Then, I remembered the door pushed open, allowing anyone from inside to get out in bad weather when snow blocked the door from moving if it was opened the opposite way.

I shoved it open, the black of the stairwell making me stop short. I stepped inside, allowing only a few seconds for my eyes to adjust to the sudden dimness of light. Dear God, please let Logan be okay.

I took a tentative step forward, lifting my skirts with one hand to free my feet from the hem, and pressed my other hand to the stones to steady myself. No railings...

Round and round I went, passing tiny alcoves every six stairs or so where guards would sit with their arrows pointed toward the enemy. The last one I passed, I swore a shadow moved. Like the shadows of the darkened stair that led to the secret chamber. The shadows that always stayed just on the peripheral of my vision, not wanting me to see. Haunting me.

When I turned to look, I lost my footing, or was that a hand on my back? A gentle shove. Its result was anything but soothing.

I cried out, hands shooting out to grab onto something, anything. But there were no handrails, not even a rope strung up with iron hooks against the wall, and my skirts... They were so long, my feet tangled up in them. I pitched forward, my knee slamming into the edge of step and then my shoulder bashed against the wall. I cried out, rolling down the stairs, body parts hitting, head smacking, and nothing to stop me from falling the rest of the way.

When the movements stopped, I was so dizzy, head swimming and every inch of me crying out in pain. I had to have broken something, had to be dying. Then again, I felt pain so I couldn't have broken my neck.

I stared up at the swirling dark ceiling. Jerked my gaze to the left where the stairwell curved. There was the shadow, coming closer. Not imaginary. But very much real.

And then I remembered nothing.

I don't know how much time had passed, but when I opened my eyes, I was lying on the softness of my mattress, vision blurred and body screaming out in agony. I blinked my eyes rapidly, taking in the orange glow of candles and a fire in the hearth. Gray blobs resembled bodies—standing, sitting, talking. People were in my room.

My entire head roared with pain, thumping in a mean way inside my skull.

But I was alive.

"...only a dozen stairs or so, she was lucky." The sound was a male voice, and I blinked trying to bring to memory who it was.

I knew it from somewhere. Knew him. But I couldn't place it. Couldn't place any name, except... Emma. That was me. And Logan. That was my...

I opened my mouth tried to speak but no sound came. I lifted a hand, trying to reach out, but I couldn't make my fingers work.

"She's awake." A grayish blob of human form hovered over me.

"What—" I started to say, my voice sounded foreign and distant, echoing in my own head.

"Hush, darling." It was an older woman's voice, and for a moment, I thought for sure it had to be my mother. Sounded so much like her. A hand brushed over my forehead, soothing as it pushed the matted, sweaty hair from my temples. Reminded me of when I'd had the flu as a young girl and my mother had sat vigil at my bedside, wiping my forehead with cold cloths and holding a cup of lemon-honey tea to my lips.

"No," I said, shaking my head. My mother was dead. Gone. This was not home. This was Gealach. The vision of the rider flying like the wind over the moors pressed in on me. "Logan... where is he? What happened?"

"Shh..." the woman said again.

I blinked open my eyes, trying to adjust them to the light in the room, but it felt so bright and made pain sear across my forehead. From what I could tell, it was Agatha sitting beside me.

"No, I won't. Stop shushing me," I whispered, the frantic words taking away a lot of my energy. "Tell me, have I broken anything?"

Agatha leaned forward, wiping at my brow again. "Not that we can tell, lass. You're badly bruised all over from your fall, but it looks like the worst of it is just sprains. Ye were verra lucky. Verra lucky indeed."

I sighed, swallowing, suddenly feeling so hot, then cold again.

"Your body is working hard to repair itself."

I nodded, allowing my eyes to rest a moment and hoping when I reopened them, that the blurriness would have ebbed.

"My lady," Ewan's voice sounded from somewhere to my right.

I rolled my head to the side, blinking open my eyes and seeing his blurry form. Or at least what I thought was his blurry form.

"Ewan," I said. I held out my hand. "Come closer."

He stepped closer to the bed, his hands clasped behind his back.

"Where is Logan?" I asked.

"He is on his way to the king, my lady." His voice was calm. Too calm.

"But the rider... Who was he?"

He cleared his throat, and when he spoke his tone was clipped. "We shall speak when ye're feeling better."

I shook my head, the motion making me all the more dizzy and my stomach rolled. I pushed up on my elbows, my head lurching forward against my chest, suddenly certain I was going to vomit on myself.

"Ye must have rest, my lady. We'll talk of the messenger when ye're feeling better. For now ye must concentrate on your health. The laird will have my head if ye're not well upon his return."

I closed my eyes, swallowing down the bile rising in my throat. I heard his words, but I heartily disagreed. I didn't want to wait. Didn't need to. As much as I wished Ewan was my older brother reincarnated, brought back from the dead, I knew he wasn't, and I didn't want him to treat me that way. Bossing me around. Keeping information from me when I needed to hear it. I...

I turned to the side, gagging, and there was Agatha again, stroking my hair and holding a pan beneath me as I retched. Very little came out as I'd not eaten yet that day. And when the gagging stopped, I was sweating all the more, my breathing ragged, stomach painful.

"I've posted guards outside her door," he said, speaking as if I weren't there. "Dinna let…anyone in, unless ye've sent for them."

His cryptic words were indicative that he thought Isabella could have been responsible for my fall. Or was I just reading into it. Had I mentioned in my unconscious state that there had been a shadow hovering above me. Was Isabella the one who pushed me? I vaguely remembered feeling that shove on my back. Or was it all my imagination?

When Ewan opened the door, I swore there was a flash of Isabella's dark smile from the corridor. A shiver stole over me. Though I had no proof, I was acutely aware that the woman wanted me dead, and that she'd tried to make it happen earlier.

The door closed tight and I was relieved to know that guards stood outside. Isabella couldn't get to me while I lay here, not without getting through them first, and there was no way she could knock out two guards that weighed twice as much as her.

Was there? I gave a mental shake of my head. No. There was no way.

CHAPTER TWELVE

Logan

The king's guards made us wait outside in the cold, the beginnings of a storm brewing from the scent of the wind. Night had fallen hours before, and the moon was high in the sky, but guarded by misty clouds.

Torches lit the battlements of Falkland Palace. The groggy guards who sat on the wall-walk were none too pleased with our arrival, but I'd pushed us hard and had no plans whatsoever to make camp outside the walls of the palace. We were in need of a hearth, ale and warm food.

"Open the doors. 'Tis Logan Grant, Guardian of Scotland."

The men peered over the side, their eyes squinting in the smoke from the torches. "Looks like ye," one of them said.

"Likely because 'tis," I drawled out.

"Ye'll have to drop your weapons, Guardian or nay," the other man said taking a sip of something that steamed in his mug.

I rolled my eyes toward my men. "We'll disarm in the courtyard."

The king's men seemed to chew on that for a moment, whispering back and forth, but then they both nodded. "A minute, then, good sir."

The sounds of the portcullis chain being cranked broke the otherwise silence. As it was raised, the doors were opened and we rode slowly into the courtyard, arms upstretched.

The king was on high alert, it would appear. I'd never been subjected to such scrutiny before.

We rode toward a brazier lit high with logs in the center of the courtyard, and boys from the stables came rushing forward to greet us.

"Disarm," I issued the order to my men.

We dismounted and worked to remove our weapons, making a pile of them in the center of the horses.

"See that these are put in a safe place, lad, and I'll see your belly full," I called to a young man standing to the side. He nodded eagerly, hunger making his cheekbones sharp and eyes wide.

My brother was fond of depriving his servants, preferring they be hungry and needy, grateful for the scraps he might toss their way. His method disgusted me.

"Why've ye come so late?" a guard asked, skulking up to us and placing himself in our path to the castle entrance. His eyes held suspicion. He wore a thick cloak of wool and fur, his bushy brows were pressed together in a frown and his beard was long and braided. Whisky flowed from his breath. There was a sneaky look about him that turned my stomach. I supposed the night watchmen were all of a darker sort given they lived without the sun, but this man was treading dangerously close to the edge of my patience.

I cracked my neck and flexed my fists, a silent warning that though I'd put my weapons aside, I was still deadly. "I've come to seek an audience with the king. We were close enough I saw no reason to make camp outside the walls."

The guard grunted, studying me with contempt. I sneered back at him and took several menacing steps forward until we were nearly nose to nose.

"Dinna look at me like I'm the dirt beneath your gutless boots. I'm the Guardian of Scotland and would see ye flogged by my own hand if ye dinna give me the respect I deserve."

The man swallowed, his lips thinned, but still he said naught. Nor did he move.

I bared my teeth, "Step aside."

He sucked his tongue over his front teeth as if trying to decide whether or not it would be worth it to get into a brawl with me. Probably the most entertainment he'd have seen that day, if not all week. But if he was smart he would have realized it was a feat he could not win and one he would walk away with more than a few mere bruises from.

Men started to gather around us. Servants, guards, a few drunken lords. Everyone was in a bloodthirsty mood, hoping we'd go at it. A few called jeers, but I ignored them all.

Irritation shot its way through my veins, making my breathing heavier, my fingers itching to curl around his neck. I wanted *him* to egg me on, not the crowd. Just to make one move that would have me retaliating. One tempting shift in his gait. I needed the fight. Needed to let out all the frustration building inside me. I'd beat him to a bloody damned pulp.

Maybe that's why my man Robert said in a low whisper, "My laird," attempting to pull me from the anger that I so desperately wanted to unleash on this man who dared challenge me.

The guard, perhaps seeing that as his own way out, held up his hands and took a few steps backward. "No need to get your ballocks in a shackle, my laird."

I straightened, taking in a deep breath that I'd hoped would calm me, but it did not. I was still furious. And I didn't think that fury would leave me until I knew that Emma was going to be mine for good, Lady Isabella was far north and MacDonald was rotting in his grave.

I stared the man down a few more moments, the tension in the courtyard crackling around us. But I'd more pressing issues than starting a courtyard brawl, as much as I wanted to. I turned from the guard and with a nod of my head, indicated for my men to follow. Upon entering the castle, the men were taken to the barracks to catch a few hours of sleep before the castle bade them rise, and I was given a private chamber on the second floor.

"I wish to see the king first thing in the morning," I informed the steward who lead me to my lodgings.

The man nodded. "I shall see that he is informed upon his rising. Though I must warn ye, Laird Grant, the king is not well at all."

I'd noticed him coughing while at Gealach, but summed it up to a case of ague that often hit many in the winter. "Explain," I said.

"He's taken to his bed early the past several nights and has been hiding the fact that he's had a fever. He's not been himself since the defeat with the English at Solway Moss. His Majesty is much disturbed by the unrest with his uncle. Henry VIII's break with Rome… The king fears we are all doomed."

I narrowed my eyes. "Dinna repeat your thoughts to anyone else. They could be the cause of more unrest amongst our people," I warned. "And the fever, how do ye know this?"

"His gentleman of the chamber has informed me, my laird."

I nodded. "The king has his pride."

"Aye, my laird."

"Has no one sent for the healer?"

The steward shifted his eyes as if expecting someone to come upon us. "I sent for the healer myself, but the king turned the old woman away this evening."

"I shall talk to him about it in the morning." Dear God, was the king so far gone that he would refuse assistance from those who could heal him? Did he wish death upon himself? 'Twas not like James at all.

"And the queen? How is Her Majesty?"

"She has taken to her childbed at Linlithgow Palace. The birth of our country's prince is expected any day now."

And I prayed 'twas a prince, for if Mary de Guise birthed another dead prince or a princess, MacDonald would have even more incentive to pounce on the throne. 'Haps the king's ague was timed with her childbed. Was it possible my brother did not have faith in his wife's ability? That he could glean that much from thin air and run with it?

"Let us pray for her and the future prince," I murmured.

The steward nodded, his eyes cast toward the floor and every doubt he had mirrored on his too open face.

"The king, dinna forget I want to see him first thing in the morning."

The steward nodded and backed from the room. Once he'd retreated, I barred the door, trusting no one in James' midst not to try and murder me in my sleep. My position and my holdings were much coveted, as was the much guarded secret I possessed. If they knew exactly what it was I held, they'd run from me, for I was strong, powerful and if I were to be king, my enemies would not survive the hour of my claim.

Lucky for them, I had no plans to take the throne for myself. The life of a king was not for me. In that, James and I saw eye to eye. I'd once wondered, questioned, even damned the king and queen for taking my birthright, but since knowing Emma, I was positive deep down that I was where I was supposed to be.

As much as I believed I'd be a better king, I wasn't. My duty was to guide my brother through his reign.

But damn, what was wrong with him now? Why refuse the healer? Why hide his illness?

Was James truly so concerned over our uncle's break from Rome and insistence that Scotland do the same? I highly doubted that was the case. James did not waffle. He either saw the merit in a move—whether or not it was right—and went with it. Or he didn't.

Henry VIII was for certain a lunatic in my eyes, but that did not make me feel the need to jump through the rabbit hole of insanity with him. And that there, was probably the best reason for me not to be king. I saw no need to worry over another monarch's personal choices and ruination of his country.

Why would James let that pressure get to him? He'd fought hard to keep us in our own, away from England.

I frowned. Indeed all I wanted at this very moment was a chance to be in Emma's arms. To marry the woman I loved and to live in peace. Knowing I would never get the latter only made me crave knowing she was mine forever even more.

I flicked my gaze around the room and blew out a frustrated breath. The room was rich, opulent, and far more than I needed. The windows were covered in stained glass and even the porcelain pitcher and bowl left for washing were gilded around the rim.

I disrobed, removing the hidden weapons I'd not taken off in the courtyard and sent up a word of thanks to the heavens for not having the surly guard search us to make sure we didn't carry concealed weapons. With as much tension surrounding this court, the king and myself, I was not about to walk around unarmed.

Didn't take much before I strapped blades back onto my wrists and thighs. I climbed into bed, arms behind my head. I'd slept armed to the teeth before, tonight would be no different.

Eliza Knight

Except that I barely slept before streaks of gold seeped through the paned glass.

Morning. A dull ache thudded at the base of my skull and my eyes felt heavy, but there'd been too much on my mind to sleep. I'd gone over in my head at least four hundred times what I would say to the king. He had to answer in my favor, there was no other reaction I'd accept.

It was very possible that if he didn't agree with me, all hell would break loose.

I climbed from bed and dressed quickly, splashing water on my face and through my hair. The liquid chill helped slightly with my headache, but I feared the pain would not cease until I was home with Emma.

Opening the door to my chamber, I could have been the only one awake, given that all was quiet and the corridor cloaked in darkness. No torches had been lit as yet and there were no windows. I ducked back into my room and grabbed the candelabra from the table, lighting the candles with a flint. A little bit of dark was not going to keep me in my chamber. Nor was the lack of human presence. I needed to have words with the king. Now.

Throughout the night visions of more marauders attempting to lay siege to Gealach haunted me. I pictured their distorted, demon bodies leaping over the walls, and swimming unseen to the water gate.

What if Gregor never made it back in time to warn Ewan? What if Isabella roamed the halls waiting for the right moment to strike? What if she somehow managed to get into the store rooms and drugged all the whisky, wine and ale? The entire castle would fall ill to her will.

I shook my head as I glanced up and down the deserted corridor. That last notion was a bit ridiculous. The woman could not have acquired that much poison. But then again, I had no idea what she used. A question I should have gotten answered

127

Dark Side of the Laird

before coming here, but it was unlikely that she would have answered in any case.

Stepping further into the hallway, the candles lit several feet around me, and I made my way back toward the stairs, still surprised not to see anyone on the stairs as I descended. On the short walk to the great hall I heard voices, that of a few servants. Upon entry, I noted several of the king's servants were about, but not as many as I would have thought at dawn.

I stopped one, a woman, grabbing her arm. "Where is everyone?"

She swallowed looking up me, some recognition in her eyes. Good, at least she knew who I was.

"Are ye wanting to break your fast, Laird Grant?" she asked.

"I'd prefer to share it with King James."

She swallowed again, her limbs trembling and I removed my hand.

"He's not at all well, my laird, and so ye see, they've not ordered a meal, but if ye like, I can have Cook bring ye some porridge?"

I grunted. "Where is the steward?"

Her eyes lit up, as though she were excited for having better news for me. "He's with the king."

My frowned deepened. "The king has risen."

"Aye, my laird."

Why wasn't I summoned? "I wish to have words with him. Please take me to his chamber."

The light went out of her eyes and she shook her head, glancing back toward the ground, her knuckles turning white against the handle of the bucket she carried. "I canna, my laird."

"Why?" The words came out harsher than I intended.

"Because he has ordered all of us to stay away." The woman's voice had gone softer, barely audible.

128

I held in the growl of frustration that bubbled to the surface. "Then tell me where his chamber is and I'll see myself to it."

Panic struck her then as she glanced up at me, her eyes wide with fear. The bucket in her hand shook as she trembled, and I admit to being worried that whatever it contained would spill on my boots. "I canna, my laird, I'm so sorry."

"Why?" I growled, not able to hold it in, and no longer caring that I sounded harsh.

"He has not told us where it is," she said, shrill.

"Ye mean to tell me that ye dinna know which room your king sleeps in?" 'Twas ludicrous!

She shook her head. "We dinna. He changes every night."

"Who knows then?"

"Just the steward."

I narrowed my eyes, a myriad of thoughts going through my mind. Was she lying? Was the steward in league with MacDonald, wishing to keep the king hidden away, vulnerable? Was he really ill or had he been poisoned? If Lady Isabella could have so easily poisoned myself and my men, wasn't it possible that someone could have gotten to the king and done the same thing?

Very possible.

I needed to find him immediately. I waved the maid away who breathed out a sigh so filled with relief, it almost made me laugh. Almost. If I wasn't so worried over my brother I might have.

As I reached the bottom of the stairs, prepared to begin my search, the steward appeared, as if from nowhere. Melting from the shadows like a spy. I narrowed my eyes, scrutinizing him, but he smiled brightly, as if I'd handed him a purse full of gold coins.

"Good morning, my laird."

"Where is the king?" I had no time for niceties.

"He is dressing now, and will meet ye in his study. Will ye follow me please? I will take ye there to wait."

I didn't move. "He has improved?"

The steward's gaze shifted slightly. "Indeed, he has. Will ye follow me?"

I nodded, trailing the steward across the hall to opposite set of stairs, but keeping extra alert to anything afoul. He led me to a chamber with a lit fire, a long trestle table and reams of rolled parchment. Looked to be the king's study, but even still, I was suspicious.

"How is King James feeling this morning?" I asked, more direct this time.

"Much better. He woke up...jovial. When I informed him ye were here, he requested that I bring ye to the study. He is most...eager to see ye."

I narrowed my eyes, studying the man. "Is he?" Something about the steward's voice was off. Was it nerves?

The steward poked at the fire and seemed deep in thought. Then he turned quickly toward me. "Aye, he is. Should ye like some porridge and ale brought? Of course ye would."

He spoke quickly, pressing his hands together and flicking his eyes all about the room, answering his own question instead of waiting for my response.

"Steward —"

"I'll have one of the maids bring it." He cut me off and took long strides to the door, but I wasn't going to let him get away that easily. My strides were longer.

I slammed my hand against the door, closing it and glared down at him. "What are ye about?"

"What?" he asked nervously, taking a short step backward. He looked ready to bolt.

I crossed my arms over my chest, standing guard in front of the door. "Why are ye acting so suspicious?"

"Suspicious?" The man shook his head and appeared to work hard at pulling himself together. "Apologies, my laird. 'Tis simply some news we had this morning. Ye see the king is a father once again."

"The queen has given birth?"

"Aye." The steward shook his head, looking disappointed. "We received the news shortly after your arrival."

"And?"

"A girl, my laird. A princess." His lips curled down, as though the words soured his tongue.

Mo chreach. I gave a curt nod. "I shall give the king my congratulations."

"Hmm. Ah, aye, indeed. If ye would please excuse me."

I nodded, wondering just how badly James was taking the news of a princess instead of a prince. If Emma were to bear me a son or a daughter, I'd be most proud. I'd be ecstatic, either gender. A sweet princess with Emma's fiery hair and pert nose. Or a strapping boy ready to give me hell. Any child was a blessing.

But not for James. Not when he'd seen his princes breathe their last within minutes of being born. Not when he needed an heir so badly to prove to the realm that he should be their true king.

The steward took advantage of me being deep in thought and pressed his hands to the door, pulling it open a few inches. "I'll have a maid bring ye some food." He skirted around me, slipping into the opening.

I grunted and turned toward the sideboard, pouring a dram of whisky as the steward pulled the door closed behind him. The distinct click of the lock had me barreling forward and yanking hard on the iron handle.

It wouldn't budge.

"Open this door!" I bellowed, ramming my shoulder repeatedly against the wood and feeling the thickness of it shudder beneath me.

But no one released me. No one uttered a word.

CHAPTER THIRTEEN

Emma

I was inside a void.

Darkness, cold and miserable, surrounded me where I stood. I wasn't in bed. I didn't appear to be clothed, but naked. Drafts of air washed up my bare legs, over my abdomen and swirled around my neck, choking me. I reached up, desperate to stop whatever it was that held me pinned, but there was nothing but a breeze.

My demons had taken me once more.

A shiver stole up my spine and gooseflesh covered my arms and legs. I walked, barefoot on a damp, stone floor. I reached out my hands, feeling nothing but the dank air, like walking through a fog at midnight, except I didn't even have the stars or moon to guide me. There was nothing but darkness.

I took a few steps, sliding my feet over the stone. It was slick, like it was covered in dirty water, and patches of algae.

Almost like the stones I'd stepped across at the lake where my family vacationed. One wrong stride and I'd come crashing down.

Where was I? Had I slept walked? The last I remember was my room, falling asleep after drinking a draught Agatha gave me.

Squeezing my eyes shut, I hoped I'd wake, because this was surely a nightmare. I was asleep and somehow I ended up here. But I didn't wake, instead, my surroundings became all the more real as shouts of pain and the lashings of a whip assailed my ears. Just like when I'd seen the scout beaten by Ewan at Gealach months before. A traitor he'd been, and his punishment had been brutal, deadly.

God, was I having a nightmare about that again? I'd thought to be through with them. Through with visions of torn flesh and spraying blood. I stopped dead in my tracks, willing myself to wake, to be done with the nonsense. Nothing happened. I was still standing there. Still shivering, naked in a foreign, dark corridor. The whipping and bellows still echoed.

But somehow, I knew, this wasn't a nightmare about the scout. This was different. I felt fear settle in the pit of my belly. My heart seized and beat in an erratic pace, and my breaths came quick and shallow as my panic took hold, took control.

Despite how real it felt, I knew this had to be a dream. *Only a dream*, I mouthed.

Vulnerable as I was, nude, alone in the dark and no idea where I was, taking control of my own situation gave me a confidence I hadn't felt before. A renewed strength flowed through my veins.

Maybe the only way to wake from this nightmare was to walk through it. It was a possibility that my dreams had something to show me. Some way to cope with Logan being away, or maybe it was the effect of the medicinal teas Agatha had been feeding me. Whatever the cause, I wasn't going to be able to get myself out of it.

And knowing that, taking control of that, helped me to take another shaky step forward. A single yellow dot of light glowed at the end of wherever I walked. A tunnel? A corridor in a castle?

Holding out my hands to feel for anything—and coming into contact with nothing—I took tentative steps forward, letting each slide of my foot, steady itself before taking another.

The light did not grow bigger, though I walked closer. It was tiny, like a hole in the wall. The screaming had stopped, and the only sound in the black hole where I was, was the pounding of my heart and air as it rushed in and out of my lungs.

When the light looked to be within a foot of me, I reached forward and put a shaking finger to it. A cold, metal rim. My finger pressed into it, blocking the light and I plucked it back out.

A keyhole?

I knelt down, my knees touching the slimy floor, and I pressed my hands to the wall—a wooden door—and my eye to the light.

What I saw had me recoiling in horror, jerking back and losing my balance, I fell flat on my ass, elbows jarring painfully into the stone floor.

No! It couldn't have been. My eyes were playing tricks on me. I pushed back up and put my eye back to the hole.

My mouth open in a silent scream, I stared through the metal rim, the light blinding me now. I leaned forward again, and looked.

Logan was inside, lying on a tall wooden trestle table. His arms were stretched over his head, strapped down with leather as were his ankles at the opposite end. He was stripped naked, blood oozing from wounds over his chest, abdomen and thighs.

Stripes of red marred his skin and deep purple bruising covered the parts that weren't bloody.

He'd been beaten, severely so.

His face was turned to the other side, so I couldn't see him. But I'd know him anywhere. He appeared to be alone. The single chamber was lit by torches hung on the walls. Various stands filled with instruments of torture weren't too far from him, perhaps a reminder to him when he waked of where he was. Long curving daggers, axes, metal hooks, razors, whips of various kinds, saws, things that looked like pliers and clamps. The stuff of nightmares.

But where *was* he?

Where were *we*?

Was this the king's palace? His dungeon? MacDonald's dungeon? Had he been captured after the Grant warrior had returned to the castle? Or was this just a manifestation of my fears? Logan, strapped to a table, vulnerable, gone from me.

"Logan," I whispered, fear making me tremble all over. My hands digging into the wood of the door.

There had to be a handle. I had to get to him. Had to help him. I pulled away, frantically searching the surface of the door for a handle with my hands. Even the tiny shaft of light from the keyhole didn't illuminate the door.

No handle.

It was flat, and the only marking on the door at all was the keyhole and three metal hinges on the side.

And I had no key. No tools to take apart the hinges.

Or did I?

"Oh my God," I whispered harshly, slapping at my thigh, to the leather tie that held the knife Logan had given me.

I wrenched the handle, freeing the knife from the strap and feeling the leather sag down my thigh. I twisted the end of the handle, trying to remember how Logan had revealed the key to me.

As I worked it, I leaned forward, looking into the light again, praying that what I'd seen before was gone. This was a nightmare after all. A too real nightmare.

He still lay there, quiet in his unconsciousness, his ribcage rising and falling in shaking, unsteady breaths.

"God, don't die on me," I hissed.

At last the handle clicked and pulled free. I stuffed the handle casing into my mouth to keep from losing it. Feeling along the wood for the hole with one hand, I pressed the key to the hole with the other, making the tiny dot of light disappear. The sound of the metal key sliding into the hole echoed in the pitch black corridor, and I held my breath waiting for someone to shout a warning, waiting for enemy guards to come chasing after me to steal the key and strap me to a table. But there was nothing.

Slowly, I turned the key, expecting to meet resistance, but not expecting it to work. A perfect fit, it turned, and clicked, unlocking. Seconds ticked by like minutes as I inched the door open a slit. I'd done it! I removed the key, and put the handle back in place, safe on my thigh, then slid my fingers into the opening I'd created, prepared to wrench it wide.

A loud sound, like thunder, jolted me and I felt myself grabbed by some invisible force and yanked backward through the air, through the tunnel. I screamed, reaching back for the door as I was pulled from wherever I was...

I woke in a cold sweat, a scream still on my lips as I sat bolt upright in bed.

This wasn't just a dream, it was a vision. I was certain of it. The powerful draw that Logan and I both had to each other... That magic that seemed to emanate from both of us and strung us together. The force that was whatever power was behind our joining had done this. They'd shown me where he was, and what was happening.

Logan was in trouble. I felt it deep in my bones. My entire body shook in great, convulsing tremors. My hands refused to steady themselves and my teeth chattered.

Agatha rushed into my chamber, her face full of fear, looking ready to pounce on an unseen enemy.

"What's wrong, dearie? I heard ye scream," she said, her thick accent making her words garbled.

"Logan," I whispered. In my heart I knew it was real. Still felt the awful terror that consumed me. My heart pounded so hard it hurt. I pressed my hand to my chest, trying to ease the pressure. "He's in trouble."

Agatha rushed forward, pouring a cup of watered ale and thrusting it toward me. "Drink."

I sipped at it, the sour liquid doing nothing to quell my parched throat and instead making me cough.

"Get Ewan," I demanded between hacking breaths.

"What happened?" she asked, ignoring me.

"I've…I've had a vision. You must get Ewan right away."

Agatha had gone pale, perhaps seeing the conviction in my eyes. These people were less likely to question a vision than those in my own time. They still believed in magic, soul mates and the spiritual link that seemed to tie many people together.

She nodded and hurried from the room.

I smoothed my hair with shaky fingers, and tried to catch my breath, but visions of Logan lying bloodied and bruised on that horrid table kept me from drawing decent air. That horrid room, filled with implements of torture…an executioner's wet dream.

"My lady," Ewan burst into the room, his eyes wide. "Agatha said 'twas urgent."

I nodded, pushing up on my hands to sit further in the bed, my muscles screaming from the effort, and aching from my own bruises. "Logan is in trouble. I have seen him."

"Seen him?" Ewan shook his head, eyeing me like I'd grown a third head. This warrior did not so easily believe as Agatha had.

"A vision," I said, my breath catching as every bruise and stripe of lacerated flesh on Logan invaded my mind. I slid my hand discreetly to my thigh, squeezing the dagger strapped there. A momentary fear that my dream had taken it from me, had me panicking for a split second. But it was still there, burning a spot on my skin. But I knew that someone had seen it, now. Agatha. Maybe even the healer, too. I swallowed hard, realizing I'd broken my promise to Logan to keep it safely hidden. Tumble down the stairs or not. "He's been hurt. He's been…tortured."

"Tortured?" Ewan came forward, a frown marring his face. "My lady, he is with the king. He is safe. Ye had a night terror, 'tis all."

"No, it wasn't. And you don't know where he is. You have no idea." I wanted to shout that it wasn't like he could pick up a phone and call. There was no way of knowing if Logan ever made it to the king. No way of knowing if his men hadn't been ambushed again along the road, or taken into custody when they arrived.

Ewan might think I was crazy, but in my gut I knew Logan was in trouble. And I was pretty certain of where he was. "The king has him. He is in a dungeon of some sort."

"Dinna say such things. Visions…they are…" Ewan shook his head and made the sign of the cross.

I sat up taller. "What, Ewan? Visions are what?"

"They are dangerous. And to speak about the king…"

"Logan is hurt, Ewan. Beaten, bloody. I thought he was dead until I saw him breathing."

"Dead?" he whispered. "Nay. He canna be dead. And ye dinna see him. 'Twas a nightmare. Nothing more."

Ewan paled, his jaw tightening as he stormed toward the window and fidgeted with the shutters.

I sensed he knew something, that it had to do with the Grant warrior who I saw before falling down the stairs. "Tell me."

He glanced back at me and I could see his hesitation. I widened my eyes, encouraging him to continue.

"Do ye recall what ye saw before ye fell?"

I nodded.

"The warrior, Gregor, came to tell us of an attack on Logan's men by the MacDonald warriors."

I nodded, having surmised this much already. "And..." I urged.

"They made it out fine. Two of our scouts were killed, but no other casualties other than the MacDonald men." Ewan crossed his arms over his chest, suddenly looking very stubborn. "He is fine. By now he's made it to the king."

"Ewan, in my vision, he was in a dungeon. He's... it was real. Very real. I swear it, he's in trouble. We have to go and save him." I was frantic now, trying to stare Ewan down, sending mind-control vibes toward him, but they weren't working. If anything, Ewan only frowned all the more.

"Ye're not leaving, my lady. There is nothing ye can do about...your vision. Laird Grant is fine. The king respects him, honors him with his position as Guardian. He wouldn't harm him."

"How can you be so certain?"

His frown deepened. "I canna, but I know if there was trouble amiss—"

"What? You'd feel it? See it in a vision? I saw him, Ewan. He needs me."

I dare not tell him it looked as though I held the key to Logan's freedom.

"Ye're not going anywhere." Ewan turned and stormed toward the door.

"You're no better than the enemy," I called out.

That stopped him in his tracks. He turned back slowly toward me, and for a moment I wished I hadn't uttered those words.

"I know ye only speak from fear, lass. I love Logan as though he were my own flesh and blood. I would never see harm come to him."

"Then we must go to him."

He shook his head. "Nay. We remain here. As he instructed." And then he was gone, closing the door behind him with no further thought to my fears. No further thought of Logan's safety.

But I didn't give a shit about his denial. I wasn't going to leave Logan to rot in a dungeon. Not when there was something I could do to save him. What exactly that was, I had no clue, but I figured when I arrived, I'd know. Fate would lead me as she had so far.

I threw back the covers, the sudden chill of the room paralyzing me for a moment. When I'd recovered from the shock, I pulled my legs over the side of the bed, feeling my muscles scream from lack of use. How many days had I laid in this bed, under the influence of whatever was in the tea?

Putting my feet on the floor, I wiggled my toes, clutched the edge of the bed and pushed myself up. My legs were weak, and it took a few moments to feel as though I could hold myself steady. Taking a tentative step forward, tingling prickles shot from my unused feet up to my hips.

I managed to make it to my wardrobe without falling, feeling my muscles grow stronger with each step. I opened the doors and rummaged around the bottom for a bag, finding a leather satchel at the bottom. I pulled it out, tossing it behind me onto the bed, then grabbed a gown, a chemise and my cloak.

I must have turned too quickly, because I was suddenly weary and my vision blurred, little black dots floating before my eyes. No! Not now! Why couldn't Fate make me immune to such base human responses?

I stumbled toward the table, hoping a sip of ale might help to steady me. When I reached it, I clutched the edge to steady myself, and then I saw the tea cup, little black bits of something on the bottom. I picked it up and sniffed it. What was that? It wasn't tea leaves.

I wasn't an herbalist in the least, but it smelled spicy, sweet and tangy. Not at all what I thought the usual medicinal herbs smelled like.

My knees buckled, and I caught myself on my elbows on the table's rim, dropping the tea cup and hearing it clomp against the floor.

Was it possible I'd been poisoned?

But who would —

I knew exactly who would. The same person I suspected knocked me down those stairs.

CHAPTER FOURTEEN

Logan

*T*he lock unclicked and the door to the king's solar banged open. Half a dozen guards, armed to the teeth, filled the small space. I bolted out of the chair I'd been brooding in, coming to stand in the center of the room, every muscle coiled, ready to pounce.

"Logan Grant, Laird of Gealach, Guardian of Scotland. Ye are hereby being held for suspicion of treason against His Majesty, King James V of Scotland and remanded to the dungeon until further investigation."

I clamped my teeth tight in an effort to not have my jaw hang slack at the ridiculous words I'd just heard spewed. Crossing my arms over my chest, I raised a brow at the guard who'd said the words, a man I'd not seen before, though I recognized the night guard who'd challenged me standing two to the left of him.

"On what grounds?" I asked, keeping my voice as calm as I could.

"Treason," the man repeated.

Not an accusation any man wanted to hear. A shiver of dread raced over my spine. To say I was stunned, well... I wasn't surprised that someone had made the claim, but I was a bit shocked that James believed it. "But I've never been anything other than loyal to King James. What treason have I caused?"

The guard ignored me and unrolled a parchment in his hands. "Ye are stripped of your title of Guardian of Scotland. Gealach Castle will remain in the king's trust until such time as he sees fit to return it to ye or give it to another."

"On what grounds?" I said again, louder this time, taking my hands from my hips and fisting them at my sides, touching the tips of the blades at my wrists with my middle fingers. Thank God I had the foresight to keep my weapons on me.

"On the words of a witness." The guard rolled up the parchment and stuffed it into the breast of his jerkin, as though he feared I'd lunge forward and rip it from his hands.

"What witness?" I pronounced the words slowly, clearly.

"If ye wish to object to these accusations, ye will be given a chance, but as it stands, ye are to come with me. Now."

Trying to remain calm, I addressed the leader of this nefarious group of king's guards. "I beg your pardon, good sir, but I believe ye have been misinformed. I am but the king's humble servant and nothing more."

"Nay, Laird Grant, there has been no miscommunication." The man braced his stance and glared at me, an edge of fear in his eyes. "Your accuser has told me himself."

I narrowed my eyes. "Who?"

"I am not at liberty to discuss that with ye at this moment. Men," he addressed those behind him, who walked around the head guard and toward me.

"Was it MacDonald?"

The man's eyes shifted, and ignored me, signaling to his men once more.

I spread my legs, battle ready. "Dinna come another foot closer," I warned. "Else ye want to kiss your arse goodbye."

But they did not heed my warning, and so I was forced to show them exactly how foolish a move it was. I lunged forward, fist connecting with one man's jaw before swinging in a circle and connecting my opposite fist with another face, and my foot kicking out to strike a man's groin. I wasn't going down without a fight. I wouldn't stand for false accusations.

The head guard called for more men, and those who were present ripped their swords from their scabbards. With thumbs up my opposite sleeves, I unhooked my daggers and dropped them into my palms, ready for whatever they were going to bring toward me.

If I'd not known better, I might have thought I'd been mistaken for someone else or that some tremendous misunderstanding had occurred. But I knew MacDonald and his tactics. And I now grasped why James was willing to issue such an order. MacDonald would have the king thinking I was a traitor, and James had so much paranoia when it came to me, that he would allow himself to believe it because it gave him a reason to be rid of me.

Since that was undoubtedly the case, I wasn't going down without a fight.

"Dinna be shy, lads," I growled.

The cocky bastards grinned as I imagined an overconfident pack of wolves would at a victim of prey they'd cornered. It only spurred me on further. I loved a challenge.

I lifted my blades and took a menacing lunge forward. For a breath they backed away, realizing that they were about to sustain some serious injuries, but, as any warrior, they had to continue with their duties and so they sank back in. The guards came at me from all sides, slashing with their swords. I blocked more than half, but the others were able to slice into me.

Pain blazed from my shoulders, biceps and back but I blocked it out.

They'd most likely been given orders to take me to the dungeon alive, for none of the wounds I sustained were more than a minor slice, but they stung like hell. Just because they'd been told to leave me alive didn't mean I had to show the same courtesy. Och, hell, no, I was taking them down. Sliced one man clear across the throat. Another, I stabbed in the heart. I slashed and connected with plenty of limbs. I ducked, spinning on my haunches and slashed at men behind the knees.

One of them, must have decided they'd had enough, for something large and heavy bashed me on the back of the head. I stumbled forward, rage fueling me to continue fighting, even as I lost my footing. I slashed at them on my knees, swinging my arms around in order to strike at anything, anyone, within hitting distance. The heavy object smacked into my skull again, rattling my teeth. I tasted blood. My vision blurred. I swayed forward and fell, but quickly rolled onto my back and continued fighting. No one could ever say I'd been taken easily.

The head guard, the one who'd told me I was to be stripped of my title, lifted a chair over his head—presumably the one he'd hit me with before. I lifted my foot to block the blow, but it didn't matter, several men held me down and I watched the back of the chair crash toward my face.

*P*ain blazed a fiery path from temple to temple, and radiated down my neck. Arms stretched up over my head, legs stretched out below. I yanked, restrained, and the straps that held me dug deep into my flesh. I was naked and weaponless. Vulnerable.

I don't know what hurt more, being strapped down and unable to move, completely at my brother's mercy, or the many injuries I'd sustained.

A door creaked open, and I looked from side to side, not seeing it. The room was barren except for racks of ghastly torturing instruments. I drew in a deep breath and held it. How much would I be made to endure on the word of MacDonald? Would I be able to make my brother see reason?

James had always wanted to see me broken, now he'd have the chance to do it.

A gruff laugh sounded from behind me, and boot heels clicked across the stone floor, echoing in the space around. But I wouldn't let the fear-inducing noises, nor the torture tools get to me. I couldn't. The only way to survive this was to remain strong. To reason with my brother.

From the dank scent of things, the overwhelming tang of blood, I was in the dungeon somewhere. Deep in the castle. What had happened to my men? Were they too down here? Or worse? Had the king ordered my men killed?

"Ye've awakened."

James. My brother. Part of me wanted to feel overwhelmed with betrayal. The other part, the smarter part, had been expecting this. Though maybe not consciously. I wasn't surprised, which meant a part of me had assumed this would happen all along. He coughed, the sound echoing off the stones and sounding rough and painful.

"How fortuitous for ye, that we do not share the same face, for that alone has been what's kept ye alive all these years," he said, from somewhere away from my vision.

I cleared my throat, my insides feeling raw. My muscles tightened, pulling on the restraints as I turned to see where he was. He stayed out of sight. I tried to relax, so the biting of the binds didn't fill my voice with pain. "And now ye'd put an end to it?"

"I see no other choice." The boot heels shuffled, sounding as though he tripped.

I strained my neck, trying to see behind me, pain be damned. His shadow wavered and he was silent. Weak. Perhaps seeing himself that way, he felt now was the time to take me down. For me, strapped to a table and beaten was the only way he could be stronger than me in body, for he would never be stronger than me in mind.

"I've heard your queen birthed a daughter," I said, my voice, though strained, still carried a measure of taunt itself.

"Women are weak," James said, coughing. "But so are ye, and I will see ye destroyed."

Something crashed against the floor and James let go a string of curses. The man was even weaker than I'd originally suspected.

"Ye should have married the bitch instead of coming here," he growled, coming closer.

I drew in a breath to steady my voice. When I spoke it was loud, clear. "Never."

"Lady Isabella could have saved ye." More coughing.

"We both know that is nay true."

"Did ye wake drunk, naked?" His voice was stronger as he taunted me, bringing back memories of that horrid morning.

I closed my eyes, my suspicions confirmed in that moment, and I refused to answer. *Remember! Remember what she did to ye!* The voice inside my head bellowed out the demand, but there was no answer.

The king laughed. "Isabella has done well then. I'll draw up a marriage contract, seeing as how the nuptials have already been consummated. She'll inherit all upon your death, which will be the same hour as my own."

I bared my teeth. "I'd never agree to it."

"Ah, but ye see—" the king came closer, I felt him push against the table I was strapped to as if to steady himself. "Ye have no choice. I've taken away your power." He laughed. "How does it feel, great and mighty, Logan Grant, to have all your power stripped from ye?"

Something cold and metal pressed to my neck and James' face loomed over my own.

"Should I kill ye now?" His eyes were so like my own, but the rest of his face was a stranger to me. I'd not known our father, and neither of us our mother. Who did he take after? And who did I?

"Do it," I said through bared teeth.

"Do ye know how very long I've dreamed of your death?" James said. "Since the moment I found out who ye were. I'll never let ye survive past me." He coughed, the blade he held to my throat digging in as he lost some of his balance. A warm trickle of blood dripped over my throat.

He could kill me now. Kill me when he wanted. Or kill me by accident. My life was in his hands.

I'd known this moment was coming. Perhaps even from the time James had come to Gealach and given me the key, and his ultimatum. My life was never my own.

And now he was proving it.

"I want to feel your blood running warm and thick on my hands," James said.

A flash of Emma's face assaulted my mind. She looked frantic with worry. Her mouth moving with panic. Was it our connection? I reached out to her, wanting to comfort her, and believing in my heart that it would take a miracle for me to see her again.

When her name came close to crossing my lips, I clamped my mouth shut and turned to face my brother, my enemy. "Ye can take away my freedom, ye can take away everything, but I'll never give ye the respect ye crave. Ye're not my king."

CHAPTER FIFTEEN

Emma

I was back in that musty, dank corridor, this time lying on my back, just as I had when I fell in my chamber. Darkness surrounded me, and an eerie pounding echoed deep within my skull.

I pushed up, my hands slipping on the scummy stone, causing me to crash back down. My elbow banged painfully, and I rubbed it as I pushed more carefully back toward the door. On my knees, I pressed my hands gently to the wood, hoping it was still ajar, the way I'd left it.

No such luck. The door was closed again. All the progress I'd made before undone by the mists of time. The dagger was once more strapped to my nude thigh, and I felt it, almost like a pulsing, pulling me to unlock the door again.

I peered once more into that tiny keyhole, realizing the pounding was the sound of my heart. Through the keyhole, I could see Logan. He was still strapped to the table, still bloody and bruised, but this time he was looking toward me, like he knew I was there. His dark eyes were intense, his lips in a long firm line.

"Logan," I called out, but the sound seemed trapped in the space around me, dull and muted.

But it didn't matter, because somehow, he must have known I was there. We were together in this altered state. Not a dream, but not quite reality either. He mouthed my name. Or maybe he said it, but I couldn't hear, only witnessed the movement of his lips.

The door must have blocked our voices, though before I'd been able to hear shouts and the sound of whipping. Now there was only my own sounds.

The right side of him faced me, and his hand flexed, clenching into a fist, and then his fingers splayed out and he motioned toward me. He was reaching for me, needed me.

A desperate sense of fear clawed from within me. Logan needed me and there was nothing I could do to help him, save him.

"Emma." His lips moved and my name, spoken on his lips, was heard this time, but inside my head. Not from my ears.

I shook my head, certain I must have imagined it, but then he said it again. Now we were telepathic?

"Can ye hear me?" he asked.

It was clearly Logan's voice, and he *was* inside my head.

I nodded, then remembered, from his distance, he wouldn't be able to see such a movement through the keyhole.

"Yes," I answered, pressing my hands so hard to the door, if it were soft I'd sink right through it.

"They have me, Emma."

I swallowed, feeling my throat constrict. "I know."

His eyes burned a fiery black. "Ye're Scotland's only hope. The king...he has been...poisoned against me. MacDonald will take over and he'll side with the English, sell us for a price."

I opened my mouth to tell him about Isabella, but instinctively closed it again, pausing. Now was probably not a good time to tell him about the bitch and what she was doing. He was in enough trouble, lying beaten on a slab and having no control over anything. There he was, more concerned about his own country, too. Never had I met a man more selfless than he. I pulled the dagger from my thigh. "What can I do? I want to save you." I licked my lips, the stress of the situation taking all the moisture from my mouth. "I have the dagger. The key fits in this door. I can open it."

Logan shook his head vehemently, a feat that had to have pained him.

"Dinna use it on me. Safeguard it."

"Logan, no! I have to save you." The handle of the knife dug into my palm as I held it with an iron grip.

Logan closed his eyes, pain etched on his face, then slowly opened them. "Emma, ye canna, my love. I am beyond saving. But ye can save this country."

Tears burned the backs of my eyes. He was pushing me away. He didn't think I could help him, or he didn't want to be saved.

"I can help you. I can save you and then you can save Scotland. You are the guardian, and I'm just...just a time traveler!"

Logan laughed, the sound gravelly and pain filled. "Lass, ye're more than just a time traveler to me. And to Scotland. Ye were sent here for a reason."

"Yes, to be with you!" I argued, refusing to take up this monumental task.

His lips quirked in that way that made me feel warm inside. Logan's indulgent smile. The one he gave me whenever he knew I needed to be coddled, and reassured. But I didn't want to be coddled, nor reassured. I wanted to help him. Wanted to take him away from this horrid place.

"Emma, do ye truly believe that Fate would have ye travel back five hundred years for a tryst?"

"We are more than a tryst, Logan. I love you. I love your people. I belong here. I should have been born in your time. That's why Fate brought me back. Not so you could suffer when I can help. Not so I can watch you—" But I couldn't finish, because I couldn't say *die*. Couldn't tell him that he looked already to be on death's door. That was not why I was brought back. I refused to believe that.

"Nay, love. Fate brought ye back, brought ye to me, so I could show ye how strong ye are. Because only ye have the power to save us all."

I groaned, slapped at the wooden door. "What would you have me do? I can't leave you here to die." And there I'd said it. That horrible word that meant he was gone from me forever. Oh, yes, his spirit would live on, but I didn't want to live on in the physical sense if he was but a spirit.

Again Logan seemed to hold his breath, his eyes closing. How much pain was he in? I couldn't even imagine. He looked... shredded. "Ye must confide in Ewan. He will help ye. Dinna linger, love, for the night grows dark and bleak."

I tried to respond, but the loud boom, like canon fire erupted, and I was once again yanked with forceful invisible hands backward, away from Logan, perhaps for the last time.

Seconds later, hands were sliding beneath my shoulders and hauling me to my feet. I blinked open my eyes, feeling groggy, my head pounding. A guard carried me back to my bed and Agatha screeched in the background.

"I dinna know how she fell, I was only gone but a second, and now she's on the floor. Oh, dear, Lord in Heaven..." And on and on she went.

"Agatha," I managed to rasp. "I'm fine."

I sank beneath the covers, shivering uncontrollably, feeling numb, cold and filled with fear.

"Dearie, ye're not fine. Why I—"

"Agatha, I need Ewan. Now." I don't know how I did it, but I managed to fill my voice with all the power I didn't feel and it came out in a rush.

She shook her head and put her hands on her hips. "Nay. Not this time. I must—"

"You *must* get Ewan. Bring him to me now. It's an emergency." I glanced toward the table, recalling the herbal tea and the cup that lay somewhere on the floor. I leaned forward and motioned to her, keeping an eye on the guard. If Agatha had done the deed of seeing me drugged, then I could yell for him to help me. I whispered in her ear, "I've been poisoned."

Agatha let out a gasp that sounded as though she might have a heart attack. She took hold of my shoulders, her eyes wide. "My lady, how?"

"In my cup. It was an herb of some sort, I'm almost sure of it."

"What kind?" Agatha glanced around the room.

"I don't know. I dropped the cup over there."

My maid turned on her heel and rushed to the table. She ducked from my sight, but I could hear her rummaging around on the floor. She hopped up a moment later with the mug in hand, and sniffed it loudly before recoiling.

"My God, ye're right. I dinna know what it is, but for certain, 'tis not tea in your cup." Agatha frowned into the cup then held it at bay before slipping it in her apron. "I'll ask Cook to help me figure it out."

"Okay," I said. "But send Ewan. Please."

Agatha nodded. "Guard, keep an eye on Lady Emma. I will go and find Ewan myself."

The guard nodded, and shut the door behind Agatha's retreating figure, hopefully to stand guard on the other side. But what if, and I was pretty sure it was Isabella, stood in the adjoining room?

I slid my hand over the dagger on my thigh, sighing with relief that it was still there, but this wasn't a weapon I could use in my own defense, not if I wanted to keep it safe. As it was, it was very likely Agatha and the healer knew I wore a dagger on my thigh, though neither of them probably knew what it was for. I glanced around the room. Nothing but a couple of candlesticks and a wash bowl. I'd be dead in a second if someone came in with a blade.

I had to get into Logan's room. Even if Isabella hid in there, I couldn't just sit here without a means to protect myself. He had an arsenal hidden in there.

This time, I took it slow. Pushed back the covers and swung my legs over the side. I let my toes touch the floor, adjusting to the coolness of the wood planks. I wiggled my toes and pressed them against the wood. They tingled at first, threatening to take away my power to walk, but within a minute or two I felt strength filling my feet. I stood, my legs wobbly. I shuffled to the foot-post, holding tight to it, and letting my legs become accustomed to standing. I wasn't going to risk what happened last time when I tried to move too quickly. There was no telling how much of the poisoned herb I'd consumed.

A few steps to the other foot-post and then back again. I practiced walking, slowly, building strength. I was dizzy as shit, but I couldn't let that get to me. I had to power through it. Logan's life, my life, and apparently the lives of everyone in Scotland depended on me being able to pull myself together.

Taking a deep steadying breath, I let go of the post and walked slowly over to the sliding door that joined our bedrooms. I slid it open, half expecting Isabella to come rushing through with a wicked dagger and murder in her eyes, but she didn't. The room was empty, dark. The light from my own chamber barely made a stripe of light in his.

But I didn't have time to light candles, I knew where I could find a blade. I lurched forward, holding my hands out to steady myself until I reached Logan's bed. His covers were cold to the touch, but straight and neat. He'd not slept there in weeks. Not since he started to share my bed at night, too.

I slid my hands over the edges, feeling my way toward his pillow, and then I reached behind the polished wood of the headboard, feeling the cold metal of several blades.

Thank God he'd shown me where his weapons were.

They all hung on hooks, specially made to store his weapons out of view. Since I couldn't see, touch was the only way to make a selection. I chose a long dagger. Shorter than a sword, but long enough I felt I could fend off an attacker who had a blade.

The handle was made of bone, and I squeezed it in my fist, feeling a little safer already.

I'd just made it through the door, back to the bed and hidden the blade beneath my pillow when Agatha came back in, a stern frown on her face.

"Why are ye out of bed again?" she asked.

"Just needed to stretch," I replied, trying to keep all emotion from my face. Logan said I was like an open book. But I couldn't be that way now, not when we were all in danger.

"My lady," she rushed forward, turning to shut the door. Wringing her hands together, she looked anywhere but at me. Then scurried over to help me get back under the covers, but I pushed her hands away.

"Where is Ewan?"

"There is no sign of Sir Ewan anywhere."

My heart leapt into my throat. "What do you mean, no sign?"

"'Tis as though he simply vanished." She shook her head in confusion and I felt the mounting dread pile heavily on top of me. "No one has seen him."

"He can't have just disappeared, Agatha. Keep looking." The words were angry, bitten out in a panic. Oh, God, had Isabella gotten to Ewan somehow?

Dead God, don't let it be so!

I pressed my hands into the mattress, steadying myself as my legs suddenly quaked, threatening to collapse.

"Where is Lady Isabella?"

Agatha frowned. "'Tis another thing... No one has seen Lady Isabella ether."

My fears were becoming realized. The bitch had done something to Ewan. I felt it in my gut. "Have the guards search everywhere. Ewan must be found within the next half hour. It's imperative." I lifted my gaze, catching Agatha's. "Our laird's life depends on it."

The maid nodded frantically and left the room.

"Logan, what am I supposed to do?" I whispered to the ceiling. "We need you."

I dropped to my knees, pressing my hands together and did something I found myself doing so much more since traveling back in time. I prayed.

And I questioned why Fate was testing us so mercilessly.

CHAPTER SIXTEEN

Emma

I don't know how many minutes went by but it felt like an hour. No hours! I sat in bed, nerves jumping and every little sound had me reaching for the blade buried beneath me. I couldn't sit still, couldn't stop the racing, panic-filled thoughts going through my mind. Staring into the flames of the candle only reminded of that tiny speck of light coming from the keyhole.

Why was it taking so long for Agatha to find Ewan and Isabella?

I let out a frustrated groan and rubbed my hands over my face. If I didn't hear something soon, I was going to go batshit crazy.

Commotion came from the courtyard. Muffled calls, nothing more, but it still made me pause. My hands stilled beside me on the comforter and I cocked my head, listening. Waiting. More of the same.

Had they found Ewan?

My stomach plummeted with a sudden fear as to what they'd found. Ewan was the only one who could help me — Logan had said so himself, and now…

Okay, stop! I couldn't let myself continue down that line of thinking. Maybe he'd just waltzed in and that was what the commotion was about.

I rushed from the bed and ignored the weakness of my body. Pure adrenaline propelled me forward. I yanked the shutters open and stared down at the crowd of clansmen forming a walking circle around something as they brought it inside. Icy wind swirled through the open window, ruffling my hair and nightgown, but my skin burned so hot, I barely felt it.

Four warriors carried a makeshift stretcher made from large tree limbs and someone's plaid. On top of the stretcher was a prone body. Golden blond hair and a broad brow peeked from beneath a plaid that wrapped tight around a man. There was only one man at Gealach with hair like that.

Ewan.

It was definitely him. I felt it deep in my bones. The same sense of loss encompassed me as it had when I lost my brother the decade before. Like a piece of me was dying with him. My eyes were wide, glued to the eerily still body of the only other man besides Logan that I trusted.

Was he…?

His head rolled the side. Either from his own movements or the jostling of his men. But I took hope that he was alive. Badly injured, but still. *Please, be alive!*

No way I was staying here to wait for someone to come and tell me what had happened. Even if I had to crawl on my hands and knees toward the great hall, I would. I had to know how he was doing, what the prognosis was. He needed a hospital, a doctor, anesthesia and modern treatments. And he wasn't going to get it.

What had Isabella done? Instinctively, I knew she was the one to blame.

Not bothering to put on a robe, I wrenched open the door, uncaring at the shocked look on my guard's face.

"Ewan is hurt," I said.

Instead of ushering me back inside my chamber, where most people thought I belonged, the guard lifted me in his arms and hurried toward the stairs.

I held on to the fabric of his shirt at his shoulders as he took the stairs down two at a time.

They'd laid him on the table in the great hall, arms splayed out at his sides. The plaid blanket had been rolled down to his waist as they examined his awful wounds. His linen shirt was torn, showing his flesh shredded and bloody beneath. Blood seeped still from his wounds, creating red polka dots on the floor. He'd been attacked. Viciously.

His eyes were closed in blessed unconsciousness. I stared at his chest, willing it to rise, and it did, but weakly. He was still alive.

The crowd of clansmen parted for my guard, and he carried me up to the table, setting me gently down. Tears blurred my vision and I blinked them back, not willing to let them impede me this time.

After lifting the arm closest to me back to his side and indicating for the blustering fool on the other side to do the same, I pressed two fingers to Ewan's neck, checking his pulse. It was faint, which I'd gathered given the tremendous amount of blood he'd lost. He needed a transfusion—something the people here would have never heard of, and I had no idea how to do it.

The world, my world, this world, was crumbling down around me in a pile of steaming shit.

"Where's the healer?" I shrieked, hearing the desperation in my voice.

Agatha pushed through the people, coming to my side. "She's coming, my lady."

"Where did they find him?"

"On the beach."

"How did this happen?"

Agatha shook her head, looking just as confused as I was. "He was stabbed."

"More times than I can count," I whispered, looking back at his quickly paling face, gray lips. If I didn't see the continual, shaky rise and fall of his chest, I would have thought he was dead. No wonder people were buried alive in the middle ages...

"Have they found *her*?"

"Not yet, my lady."

Damn... Isabella could be anywhere. I heard a guard murmur that Ewan had last been seen trying to find Isabella to confine her in her room.

"Carry him upstairs to the laird's chamber," I ordered.

"My la—" Agatha protested, but I cut her off.

"Now."

Several guards lifted Ewan and carried him toward the stairs, none second-guessing me.

"My lady, do ye require assistance?" my guard asked.

I nodded.

He lifted me once more and we, too, departed the great hall.

The healer arrived on our heels and ushered everyone from the room. I protested, but she wouldn't hear anything of it. She did, however, agree to letting Agatha remain behind. Only after my maid swore to bring me news every hour did I retreat to my own room—via the hallway. No need for the added questions of anyone who might intrude when I used the adjoining panel.

I nodded to my guard in the hallway then stepped through the door, shutting it behind me. As soon as I turned around,

Isabella stepped out of shadowed corner, a smile peeling the corners of her lips back. I sucked in a breath, pressed my back to the door as though its sturdy build would protect me from her.

"What are you doing in my room?" I hissed, anger fueling my blood to boiling.

"Waiting for ye. I suppose ye saw my warning?"

"Warning?" I crossed my arms over my chest, forcing myself not to stare toward the bed where my blade was safely hidden beneath the pillow. I'd like nothing more than to slice this bitch up.

"Your precious little puppy dog."

"I don't own a dog," I said, feigning boredom.

"Och, nay, sweet Emma, ye own nothing. This puppy follows ye around hoping for a chance to rut on ye like his laird."

I narrowed my eyes, her vulgar words so offensive and shocking they didn't register. "What?"

She rolled her eyes. "Ewan, ye half-wit."

I rolled my eyes back, with an extra oomph of exaggeration. "You're a very bad judge of character. Though I'm not surprised. Ewan is like a brother to me."

She walked over to my window and gazed outside before closing the shutters. My stomach turned in knots. Was she about to slice me up like she'd done to Ewan? How had she overtaken a massive warrior?

"Then ye sin in more ways than one," she said, a smirk on her lips.

"You think you're so clever." I took three steps forward, anger fueling the impulsive move. "But there's one thing you forgot."

"What's that?" she asked, tapping her fingers on the table near the tray where the tea cup I'd found with the weird herbs had been.

"Your warnings mean nothing to me," I ground out.

Isabella pressed her fingers to her lips, mock surprise in her expression. "Oh, dear. Poor Ewan will be so disappointed to hear that. Ye know I lured him to the beach by telling him I'd seen ye run down there." She pursed her lips, her eyes looking off in the distance, a gleam coming into them that sent a shiver careening down my spine. "Convinced a guard to go along with it." She laughed and snapped her fingers. "Off he went when I brushed my hand over his cock."

I tilted my head to the side, refusing to let her see my pain. It was hard to hide hit. Hard to act calm when all I wanted to do was rush screaming toward her and strangle the breath from her evil body. But Isabella was a rabid dog. Who knew what she had up her sleeve. So, I took a deep breath and forced myself to act as rationally as I could when I asked, "How can you live with yourself?"

Isabella looked taken aback for a mere second or two, her mouth opening a fraction of an inch, eyes connecting with mine, before she regained her composure. Like a mask, that vile person she was swiftly suppressed her brief stagger.

"The difference between you and I, Emma, is that ye care too much. Ye care too much for others, and ye care too much about your own soul." She smiled cruelly. "I dinna care for anything other than getting what I want."

"Pity, then, that I've made it my life's ambition to see that you get nothing you desire." I sneered. "Evil will not triumph."

Isabella threw her head back and laughed. A bone-chilling evil sound that made my heart leap into my throat. I was mesmerized, horrified, watching her. It was unreal. She shook her head and wiped at her eyes.

"Pity," she mocked, "that ye dinna have the power to see your pathetic threats realized."

Isabella held her hand out and wiggled her fingers, showing me the ring settled beneath her middle knuckle. It was hard to keep my mouth from dropping when Logan's ring gleamed from that long, dagger-like appendage.

"Ye see it?" she asked, her voice overly excited.

I glared at her, refusing to speak.

How had she gotten his ring?

Any trace of soul — if there'd ever been one — left her face, evil coming into her eyes, flattening her lips. "Ye're too late. Your laird is dead. Gealach is mine."

There were no words to express the severe panic and pain that wrenched itself viciously through my body. There was no other way she could have gotten his ring, than if he was dead. He never took it off, joked that it had permanently become a part of him he'd worn it so long.

I started to shake. And no amount of trying to still my trembling body worked.

"That's a forgery," I said through bared teeth as they, too, had started to chatter.

Isabella chuckled. "Ye may wish it were so, but that will not make it be."

She held it up closer, and I could see where a deep groove in the gold near the ruby had been cut — just like in Logan's. He'd sustained it during a battle, nearly lost the finger. A small detail like that... Could it have been forged? Or would something like that have been missed. Was this ring his? Was he...dead?

Numbness filled me. "Get out," I said, coldly. "Get the fuck out of here."

Isabella laughed her way to the door. Rage, raw and reckless took hold and I lunged toward the mattress, frantically searching for the blade so I could cut her throat.

"Looking for this?" she taunted, holding up the dagger. "Dinna even think," she spat, "of trying to kill me ye little bitch."

The door slammed shut behind her, and she issued orders, loud enough for me to hear, that the guard was not to let me out.

"Fucking bitch," I said through gritted teeth. Would have screamed it, but my voice escaped me.

I collapsed onto my knees upon the soft carpet at the foot of my bed. The one Logan and I had made frenzied love on more than once. I fell to my side, curled up in a ball and let the tears that I'd been fighting fall. My entire body shook with my grief. It was too late. I'd not been able to save him.

Even if he wasn't dead yet, he would be soon. Isabella had seen to that by butchering Ewan alive.

God. I was crushed, devastated. Ruined.

Logan was gone to me forever. And I'd been the one to push him away. I'd encouraged him to go seek out the king, to make his own way in this world. In essence, I'd killed him.

And Ewan. I was pretty damn sure he wouldn't pull through. Not with how mangled his body was. Almost like Isabella turned into some sort of were-creature and tore the shit out of him with her teeth. I wouldn't have been surprised if she was the devil herself.

Was she now telling everyone that Logan was dead? I was next. With Logan gone and Ewan nearly, there was nothing left here for me, and no one left to protect me from the evils of this era. Logan had asked me to save Scotland, but I… I didn't have it in me. I wasn't here for Scotland. I was here for him, and just because I'd traveled back in time didn't mean I could somehow miraculously save them all. Besides, in present times, Scotland was still around, and strong, and without me.

Or was that because of me?

Fuck! I couldn't think straight. Couldn't be made to make decisions. Logan was everything to me, and now I'd lost her.

My insides hurt, my head pounded, my heart literally ached. I clutched at my chest, knees bunched up in my middle. I might as well throw myself from the window now. Just end it.

I rushed to the window. Tore open the shutters and let the icy winter air into the room. Watched as the sun took its leave. Darkening the room and sending little comfort to my distraught mind. Everywhere I looked reminded me of Logan. Everything about this place, about even myself, reminded me of him.

As the room grew darker, the moon rose, until it was high in the sky. Round, silver and — full.

Was it a sign from Fate? Was it my destiny to now pursue that circle of stones?

My gut clenched and I squeezed my eyes shut, shaking my head. No. I couldn't go back there. The last time I'd run, Logan had chased after me, found me in those stones and punished me with pleasure, right there in the middle. Memories assaulted me from every direction. I could smell him as though he stood not a few feet away. So strong was my sense of him surrounding me, my eyes flew open and I expected to see him there, but he wasn't. Just as I'd known deep down he wouldn't be.

Without saying goodbye, I pulled on my cloak and boots and stole through the secret passage that Logan had shown me before, walking down the darkened, cobwebbed and critter-filled stairs into his library. It was dark inside, blessedly empty.

I leaned against his desk for several heartbeats, stilling my rapid breaths, resting my sore limbs. From there I made my way down to the water-gate, planning what I would say to the guards when I arrived there, but they were gone.

I swallowed hard, staring back up at the darkened stairwell and then around at the empty gate. Isabella had made sure this entrance wasn't guarded. MacDonald's men would invade at any moment, killing mercilessly.

A twinge of guilt sparked, but I couldn't stay. Couldn't die here. I had to go to the stone circle, had to find out what my destiny was. Needed to leave this place to its people.

People I'd grown to love. Walking down the cobbled stairs to the beach, and then running—lungs burning and legs threatening to collapse—was the hardest thing I'd yet done. Hard to leave these people behind. But what good could I have done them? Nothing. I wasn't skilled with a weapon and I was no use as leverage. I had no power. I was the laird's lover, nothing more.

The closer I grew to the stone circle, the stronger his scent grew in my mind. I felt him surrounding me, inside me. Was it his spirit guiding me? Did Logan want me to leave this place, too? Was he protecting me?

At last I broke through the trees and saw the stones jutting up into the moonlit sky. They glowed silver against the black of night. As before, I came forward, touching the runes upon the stone archway, which I'd thought before to be the entrance.

A burning sensation came from my hip as I touched it. I looked down, and a shaft of light glowed at the spot through my nightgown. My tattoo. The rune tattoo I'd gotten on a whim. It burned—like it had some sort of magical draw to this place.

But that couldn't be, could it?

With no one about, I lifted my gown up around my hip and stared at the tattoo. It glowed a silvery blue in the moonlight, and then all the runes upon the stones lit up before my eyes.

It was a sign.

I stepped through, sure that by the time I walked into the center, I'd be back in my own time. I closed my eyes, and when I opened them, I expected to see the cab driver waiting upon the road.

But I wasn't back in my own time.

I was in Logan's torture chamber. Candles glowing an eerie orange against the dark walls. Offensive scents of death reaching me, assaulting.

"Emma."

Logan was alive. He called faintly to me in his sleep.

CHAPTER SEVENTEEN

Emma

*T*he room was frigid, colder than outside. Gooseflesh covered my naked skin, prickling the hairs up on my arms. Puffs of air filled the space before my lips as I breathed, and my toes were nearly frozen to the icy stone floors.

But I didn't care. Logan was here. Instead of being tossed into that decrepit corridor, I'd been sent through the door.

"Logan!" I rushed forward, relief flooding me, so much so, I was light-heated, and I had to pause a moment to regain my balance.

He rolled his head at the sound of my voice, his eyes, glassy and pain-filled caught mine. I was so used to seeing the burning charcoal of his gaze, that the muted gray stunned me.

"Emma," he rasped, and his throat bobbed as he tried to swallow. His voice was so scratchy, filled with pain it sent a shudder through me.

"Oh, my God!" I cried, reaching the side of the table and clutching at his face as I pressed my lips to his.

They were cracked and bloody, but I didn't care. I was so damn thankful that he wasn't dead. Tears slid over my cheeks, mingling in our kiss. Wet warmth touched my fingertips and I realized that Logan was also crying. I swept his tears away with the pads of my fingers. I kissing him all the more. The man was already so beaten down, I couldn't bare him thinking that I thought less of him.

But feeling his tears, it made me want to sob. I had to hold myself in check. He needed my strength, not for me to break down. When I finally did pull away a couple of inches to look at him, he said, "How did ye…?"

I shook my head, kissing his cheeks and forehead, still disbelieving that I'd actually landed here, and not outside the door where he seemed so far out of reach.

"I don't know. I went to the stone circle and —" I bit my lip, refusing to continue.

"Ye were leaving?" he asked, sounding heart-broken. He swallowed again, and I couldn't find the words to answer him, because he spoke the truth, and yet to admit that I'd been deserting him, seemed so cruel.

He pressed his lips together firmly. Nodded, then in a more sturdy voice, he said, "Good, ye must go. I should nay have…"

But his voice trailed off on a crack. My own heart lurched at the emotion in his voice.

"Don't ever have regrets. I'm here, and there is nowhere else I'd rather be." And then all that had happened, all I'd sworn to keep pent up inside, came out in a torrent of words that I wished I could have held in a little longer. "Isabella said you were dead. She has your ring. She's nearly killed Ewan, I don't know if he'll make it. I was distraught, and then when I went to the circle…something magical happened."

Just as I imagined, Logan looked stricken. "We are linked, ye and I." He looked off into the distance. "Ewan was hurt?"

I nodded, unable to say all that I'd seen. "But the healer is looking after him."

Logan nodded. "I've let my people down," he murmured.

"No, no you haven't. Don't say that."

"I should have known there was a trap when I first arrived."

"How were you to know?"

"There were clues."

I shook my head again. "Don't beat yourself up, Logan. They've done that enough to you already. I'm here now. I can help you."

I still couldn't figure the whole transporting thing out. How was I here? Did *how* matter? Somehow, some higher power knew that we two should be together and tore the bounds of time to see it done. And now the bounds of space.

"But ye are nay really here," he said, looking at me so despondently I nearly crumpled to my knees. To see a man as strong as Logan brought down so low was unimaginable, heart-wrenching.

"I am here. Can't you feel me?" I pressed my hands to his face, kissed him hard and quick on the mouth. "I feel you."

"Aye, but… I know this must be another vision. Just as real as the others. The stone circle must have made our telepathy all the more potent." His eyes flicked back and forth between mine. "Are ye really here, or is this just a dream to keep me sane?"

"It's real, Logan. You had them, too?" I asked, still in shock that we were able to communicate in such a way, if indeed this was but another vision.

He nodded, then cringed in pain.

I looked down the length of his beaten body. He looked almost as bad as Ewan. Skin ripped open from crudely welded instruments of torture. Ligature marks on his neck from being stretched, and his wrists and ankles were bloody where he was bound.

My lip quivered looking at the destruction. How could someone be so cruel? How could the king have done this to his own flesh and blood? Why torture him? What had Logan ever done to deserve such treatment? "I have to help you," I whispered, enormous, hot tears rolling down my cheeks.

"Ye have to get help, for everyone at Gealach. If he's done this to me. If Isabella has gotten to Ewan... There is no telling how long before my people are made to suffer."

"What can I do? Isabella has taken over Gealach. Even when I was leaving the guards had been removed from the water gate."

I expected Logan to cringe, to swear, but he merely nodded. "The king is dying. He wants to see me dead. Every trace of me gone. They'll burn down the castle, kill everyone inside. Ye must go warn them. Allow them the chance to leave or fight back. Ye must wake now. Ye must open the secret door, Emma, and bring the treasure of Gealach to Falkland Palace. Ye must present it to the king in exchange for my life." He gave a slight shake of his head. "'Twill likely not work, but 'tis worth a try."

My body started to tremble with fear, great torrents. "No we have to go together. I won't leave without you. I can't do it without you. Can't I help you get out of these bonds?"

"You can try." But he didn't sound very hopeful.

I was determined. Try I did. I tore at the bonds, breaking my nails back, bleeding, but I couldn't get the damn leather straps to budge. "How is this possible?" I was frantic now, ripping and grappling. "I can feel you, see you, sense your breath on my cheek, and yet I can't undo these straps."

"Because, love, ye are only here in spirit." Logan's voice was calm, incredibly so. He stared up at me with pride, with love, passion, trust.

I shook my head, refusing to believe it. "No. That can't be." I yanked at the buckle again, but it was as though I didn't touch it at all.

"Ye have to go back to Gealach. Ye're the only chance this country has. But first... make love to me, Emma."

"What?" I asked, my voice breathless. Shocked at his request.

"Make love to me. Give me strength to last until ye come for me in truth."

I couldn't refuse him. How could I? This could be the last time I ever saw him. "Yes. Yes," I murmured, pressing my lips to his. Then I stared at him. "How should I do it? I can't get your bonds undone."

He grinned up at me. A piece of that wicked, delicious man still present behind the bruised outer shell. "Just like I taught ye, love. Ye be the one in control."

"No." I shook my head. "My body may be controlling yours, but I would never take away your will."

"God, I love ye," he said. "This is my will. I want ye desperately. Let me live off this memory."

I kissed him again, frantically, my body coming alive with each slide of my tongue over his. I wished he could touch me. Wanted so desperately to feel his hands on my back, my hips, my breasts. To feel the slide of his thumb over my cheek, his fingers tangling in my hair.

"Soon," I whispered, more to myself. "Soon, you will be safe."

I climbed onto the table, wood splinters biting into my knees. Logan was already hard, his cock jutting from his pelvis, rigid, stiff and a drop of moisture on the tip.

"Put me inside ye," he begged. "Please, love."

"Don't beg me, Logan. You don't beg. Logan Grant demands."

He closed his eyes, and I could see in that moment how very desperate he'd become. How broken. I needed to make him whole again.

"I want you so bad, baby," I said, straddling him, and leaning over his chest to kiss his lips. My breasts brushed against his chest, the crisp hair on his chest making my nipples pucker and burn for him. Logan hissed a breath. "Am I hurting you?" I asked.

"Nay. Ye give me strength." His muscles tightened beneath me and he shifted up, showing me with his body how determined he was.

"I want to give you everything," I whispered.

"I only ask for your heart."

I nuzzled the side of his neck. "You have it."

"I love ye," he whispered.

"I love you, too," I murmured against his lips. I kissed him deeply, passionately, hoping that every ounce of love I felt came through that kiss. Wanting to heal every wound, close every slice, mend every bruise.

I reached between us, gripping his thick cock and slid it between my wet folds, finding my center slick and ready. I pushed back, taking the length of him in deep.

"Och, aye, lass." Logan ground, his jaw clenching tight, but his eyes wide on mine. "I can feel every bit of ye. Tight, wet, hot. 'Tis hard to imagine ye're not here with me."

"I'm here, Logan. Every bit of me." I moaned, rolling my hips forward and back. I wanted to grip his chest, feel the muscles shift beneath my fingertips but I was afraid I'd hurt him, so I slowly, gently, slid my palms up his arms to his hands where they were strapped, and entwined my fingers with his. "And I won't leave until whatever power brought us together, tears me from your arms."

"Even when ye're not here, ye're here. In my heart," he said.

"Oh, Logan, you have no idea."

174

I bent forward again, kissing him as our bodies rocked. He bucked his hips, sliding in and out of me, and I matched his rhythm. With every moment we were joined, he grew stronger, as though my body gave him resilience and power.

"I wish this could last forever," I said.

"It does, lass, in our minds."

Burying my face in the crook of his neck, I felt his pulse beat against my lips. "Your heart is growing stronger."

"As I said, ye give me strength, love. Strength to keep going."

"I can't live without you." Tears welled in my eyes again.

"Dinna say that."

"But it's true."

I sensed his struggle, his body tightening, his jaw clenching. "'Tis the same for me." His voice cracked. "Bloody hell, but I want to hold ye."

Tears did fall down my cheeks then and I swiped them away. "I want you to hold me, too, so you'd better not let them kill you."

He chuckled, a weak, half-hearted sound, but when he spoke, his words were intense and powerful. "I'll try my damnedest, Emma, ye can count on it."

"With every breath I will," I said, capturing his lips in a fiery kiss. I wanted to forget this conversation. Forget that he was strapped to a table in the bowels of a castle I had little hope of getting him out of without a miracle. I didn't have a Fezzik to carry him out or a Miracle Max to heal his injuries. Ha, I wasn't a princess bride either... But it didn't matter, I had to believe in magic, that Fate would save us both.

So I kissed him hard. Kissed away the pain, the fear. Forced us both into a place where only pleasure, sensation and love reigned. And with that kiss, I rode him. Hips swaying in time with his thrusts, stopping and teasing us both with a swivel here and there. Pulling up until his cock nearly left me, and then crushing us both with a forceful push down.

Normally when I teased like that, Logan would grab my hips, steady me, and pound up inside me like there was no tomorrow. Now, when there really might be no tomorrow he couldn't do it. Couldn't make the taunting pleasure cease. But that didn't seem to matter, because in spite of how many times I paused to catch my breath, my pleasure only increased. Heart beat rapidly, breaths quick and shallow. My ears rang. My fingers tingled, and seductive ripples of the beginnings of an orgasm licked at my center.

Still, I tried to drag it out. Tried to make it last forever.

"Dinna make me wait, lass. Give me *everything*."

As always, my body was his to command. An orgasm ripped through me, likely the strongest I'd ever felt. I jolted, a deep shudder taking over, thighs clenching tight to his hips as I ground my pelvis against his. I clutched at one of my breasts, imagining it was Logan's grip on my flesh, and kept my other hand tightly squeezed with his. Wave after luscious wave lapped at my senses. Every nerve-ending sang with pleasure, and I cried out, unable to keep my pleasure hidden. Riding out my carnal bliss, I tried to keep some shred of control in order not to hurt Logan, but he bucked with frenzy upward, his cock spearing me deep as he trembled violently and called out his own cry of release.

I smiled, opening my eyes to look down on him, but all I saw was the dewy grass of dawn beneath my knees and the sacred stones surrounding me.

"No!" I cried out, leaping to my feet, turning in frantic, dreary circles. "Logan!"

But the only answering call was that of a bird cawing from a nearby tree.

"No!" I collapsed to my knees again, allowing myself a moment to grieve the loss of Logan.

I cried into my hands and prayed hard that whatever forces had helped us to be together, helped him to stay alive, too.

Dragging myself to my feet, I found my discarded garments and slowly pulled them on. Mourning the emptiness of my life without Logan readily in it.

What we'd shared was magical, spiritual, and I couldn't have been more grateful for its happening. But I didn't want it to end.

And I feared going back to Gealach.

I stared through the circle toward the pathway I'd need to take to get there. What horrors would await me upon my return?

CHAPTER EIGHTEEN

Logan

A gasp tore into my mouth with painful clarity. Parched, cracked lips. Swollen tongue. Raw, sore throat. I was severely dehydrated.

And completely fucking aware.

A flash of memory. Isabella shoving me to the ground, her vicious smile as she loomed over me, tore at my clothes. Me trying to push her away, but limbs so heavy, I barely got them off the floor. Her frowning at my cock and murmuring about how it wouldn't work. Numbness, tugging. She cursed, then she wrenched the dagger from the loop on her belt, the blade catching the light of the candle. I thought she was going to stab me. Tried to tell her not to, but no words came. The blade came down, ending on her finger, drawing blood. She smeared it on me, then stood, and hissed that she'd seem me hang. Then she faded away.

I clenched my fists, barely able to make my fingertips touch my palms. Thank God, I'd not fucked her. It was all a ruse. One she and the king had fashioned. How deep was their bond? I shivered. But not from relief or fear. My body was on fire. Fever most likely, in addition to being nude in the dank, bowels of a dungeon in the middle of winter.

But there was hope! I'd not betrayed Emma!

Puffs of steam rose from my mouth, showing just how frigid it was. The only time I'd felt warmth was when I'd envisioned Emma, an exquisite life-giving dream. Though, she wasn't here, I could still feel the warmth of her breath on my face, the light touch of her fingers on my shoulder, the heated silk of her body as she pleasured me.

Was it real?

It felt so real… and in my vision, Emma had thought it real. Even I'd convinced her that we were together in spirit. Or was it just a fantasy? The mad imaginings of a man in chains? A man with no hope of escape? Was I retreating into the recesses of my mind in order to maintain some semblance of humanity and hope?

Hope had been restored with the discovery that Isabella had not been able to fornicate with me. Oh, what vile trickery that was! She'd known I'd not remember. Knew that it would tear at my insides and had hoped that I would give in. Well, I wouldn't! Strength penetrated the dullness of my body, the power that had been stripped from me. But I knew that without help, healing, food, warmth, I'd not last many more days.

I prayed I could survive however long it would take for Emma to open the door in the secret chamber and bring the evidence of my birth to the castle. Prayed that offering up such a treasure in exchange for my life was worth it in James' eyes. Aye, James had been the one to give it to me. A test. A way to keep me close. But I'd discovered what was in there. Evidence of my birth could be the only thing.

If he wanted it opened upon his death, it could only mean that it was so I could succeed him. And now that he'd had a child born to him, I was of no use, for his line would continue even if it was daughter, and he'd not want to see it taken away from him and his blood by me — the rightful king.

A frustrated growl passed through my lips and I tightened my muscles, wrenching hard at the bindings, wishing I'd the power of the supernatural and could break free with a mere tug. But the tight straps held firm and I only succeeded in further injuring myself.

The door to the dungeon creaked open and the shuffling of feet moved slowly from where it stood ajar and out of my vision. Slow-moving, as though the person were sneaking in. There was no way it could be Emma, my jailor or James.

I wanted to shout, to ask who was there, but doing so would show my fear, my need to know. Instead, I looked up at the ceiling, and listened.

These steps were different than the rest. Slower, less agile.

"My laird," came the cooing of an older woman. Her voice was scratchy, unearthly.

Gooseflesh rose upon my limbs and I gritted my teeth. The devil's demons were upon me. He'd sent a witch to torment me and drag me down to hell.

"My laird, dinna fear me," she crooned.

I kept my teeth clenched so tight the muscle in my jaw started to spasm.

She drew nearer and I waited for the scythe to raise and gut me, but it didn't come. Instead she set something down and loomed her old, wrinkled face over mine.

"Ye're still alive, then."

"Aye," I ground out. "Have done with it and end me."

She chuckled and clucked her tongue. "Och, such a brave laird ye are, but stupid nonetheless."

"What?" I asked, staring into her dark, droopy eyes.

"I've not come to kill ye, my laird, but to save ye."

"Save me?" I was sincerely skeptical. How was an old crone going to save me? Unless she was, in fact, a witch as I'd suspected and she'd laid a sleeping spell on all who remained within the castle.

Before I'd met Emma, I might have raised a brow at such a notion as magic, but as it was, my love had traveled back in time. It was entirely possible witches were a thing of truth.

"Before ye get your hopes up, lad, I canna take ye out now. But I can feed ye and tend your wounds. Ye must remain strong, else there is nothing I can do."

"How do I know what ye feed me is nay poisoned?"

"Ye dinna. Ye must trust me. I know your secret." She hissed the last word on a whispered breath, and what was left of the blood in my body seemed to drain to somewhere, or simply evaporate.

And even though she scared the shite out of me, I wanted to trust her. Had no other choice really, for I'd no way of knowing whether or not Emma was going to succeed. If my vision had been real, I believed she would try. But there was that doubt, that it had only been the ravings of a mind gone mad.

"Ye know nothing," I insisted.

"Aye, my laird, but I do. For ye see, I was a maid to your mother. She oft told me of the two babes swirling in her belly. No one believed her, thought she was crazy, but she could feel each pair of feet. When the childbed called, she bade me hide in the wardrobe, for she was certain something afoul would happen when her two princes were born. She was right. She made me swear never to tell, but to make certain that one did not harm the other."

I couldn't respond. My jaw clamped tight. I'd known it was true, having heard so from my brother, my foster mother, but to hear it from a witness was...a blow to the gut. I swallowed and steadied my breath before answering. "Did ye know where they took me?"

She shook her head. "Nay, lad. But when I heard whisperings of ye here, I knew I had to come to ye. We've not much time now. Will ye trust me?"

"I trust ye," I said, knowing I had to do whatever it took to get out of here alive.

"Good. Now open your mouth and lift your head."

I did as she instructed, and she poured a nasty tasty elixir into my mouth. My immediate reaction was to spit it out. The last time I'd taken a drink from a woman I barely knew I'd ended up nude and unconscious. Well, I was already nude, and barely conscious as it was. What could it hurt?

Noticing my hesitation, she tsk-tsked me until I swallowed.

"That's it, my laird, drink up."

"What is that?"

"It will make ye strong. Help ye to feel no pain, for they are certain to beat ye once more."

"Why? How do ye know this?"

"The queen has birthed a daughter. They will want to silence ye and all ye know forever."

"More," I croaked. I drank down the cup of brew and then sipped at spoon after spoon of broth. My stomach threatened to recoil, to spew it all out, it had been so long since I'd eaten, but mind over matter won, and I kept it down, feeling energy renew itself in my veins.

"I'm going to put some salve on these wounds. I can do no more than that now. If I stitch ye, they'll only rip them out. The vicious hounds."

I nodded.

"Close your eyes and rest while I work. Ye're likely to be wakened soon."

I nodded again, closed my eyes, and took mental note of every part of my body, every pang. Within in moments, the pain ebbed, though my mind remained sound.

"Concentrate on healing yourself. The mind can do powerful things," she whispered as she rubbed a smelly, greasy concoction into the wounds at my wrists.

The woman worked from head to toe, rubbing one smelly ointment after another as she whispered things I didn't entirely understand. I felt myself growing stronger. Concentrated on binding the lashes in my skin back together. Healing the bruises and mending the broken ribs.

I felt better, stronger. Not whole at all, but at least I didn't feel as though death might claim me at any moment.

All the sudden, the women's hands stilled and she took in an audible breath. "They come. I must go, but I will return. I will help ye, give ye back your birthright."

"Nay! Dinna say that," I growled. By the time I opened my eyes, she was gone.

But the boot heels clicking on the floor were unmistakable. Sounded like the king's man, the one who strapped me down and implemented my brother's cruel wishes.

I kept my eyes straight ahead, not willing to show weakness by feigning sleep, and not willing to show this arsehole a lick of respect.

His welcome was a brutal lash of a whip across my belly. I couldn't even double over in pain, the straps that bound me kept me still. And thank the saints, the potion the old woman had given me dulled the pain of the lash.

"Where's the key?" he asked, rushing forward, over excited it would seem as he hovered above me, smiling and drooling like a hound who taunted his prey.

I sneered with disgust. "What key?"

He wrenched back his arm, slapping the whip down onto my thighs, only inches from my cock. Again, he received no reaction from me.

"Next one's going to hurt even more ye cock bastard, now where is it?"

"I have many keys." I closed my eyes, pretty certain of the man's reaction.

"I warned ye." The leather strap came down hard on my cock and ballocks.

I gasped, choked. Not sure if it was because I felt it or because I knew what he'd just done.

He laughed. "Told ye it would hurt. Now give me a better answer, or I'll see your ballocks pummeled until they fall off. I'll only ask ye once more. Where is the key to the secret door?"

"Gone," I forced out, proud of how strong my voice sounded.

"Gone where?" He loomed over me, the leather whip coiled around his fist and poised over my nose.

"Stolen."

"By who?"

"If I knew that, I'd have gotten it back."

God, I hated the way he cocked his fist back, threatening, as if I'd never been punched before. I wouldn't beg for him to stop. I was no coward. I'd let him beat me into the earth before I ever cowed.

"A clue, then?"

I smiled, excitement at being able to cause some manner of mischief making me feel a fleeting moment of control. "'Twas when MacDonald was at the castle. All of the Highlands knows he wants to rule, that he's been seeking the answer to secrets I hold. I'd wager my life he stole it."

"Would ye now?"

"Aye."

"Too bad I'm nay going to take your wager. The king's already ordered ye to die, ye son of a bitch."

I grinned. "And he was too much a coward to come give me the good news himself?"

I was momentarily stunned by a crack to my jaw, the bones in my face rattling and a trickle of blood seeping from the corner of my lip.

"He said I could kill ye anyway I want." My tormenter came down close, his breath fetid. "And I want to kill ye slowly."

"Will ye jerk your cock while ye do it?" I jeered.

That earned me another mind-shuddering blow. My vision blurred, and I blinked away the black dots, willing myself not to lose consciousness.

"I just might." He cackled. "And then I'll spew it in your face."

I fought the rush of nausea, and held my lips firmly in place, refusing to say another word, or show how he affected me.

"As it is, I'm a fan of twenty-two cuts," he said. "Though, in your case I'm going to add in a few extra slices, like your cock and ballocks." The metal of his blade touched my left eyebrow. "I'll start here. Take both brows off, and then the blood will drain into your eyes. 'Twill sting, I imagine. And make it hard to see where the blade goes next. But I've no shame in telling ye. I'll roll ye over and slice off the skin right here on both sides." He dragged the knife hard, cutting into my skin, along the side of my back where my shoulder blades were. "After that, I'll lop off your chest muscles, the skin on your forearms —"

Someone cleared their throat from the door, and the bastard turned away from me.

"What do ye want?" he growled.

"His Highness, sir, he's..."

The king's torturer left me, stomping over to the door where the two men whispered fiercely.

I tried to hear what they were saying, but none of it was decipherable. A few moments later the maggot returned to me and pressed the blade to my cheek, carving a burning line from the corner of my eye to the corner of my mouth. Not too deep, but enough to make me cringe and bleed.

"I'll be back for ye," he said. The man came close to my face, licking his lips, his teeth brown and eyes blazing with hunger. I don't think I was too far off in thinking he gained an immeasurable amount of pleasure from torturing people.

He came so close that for a second, I wondered if he was going to kiss me. I could almost taste the foulness of his breath as I took in one last draw of air and held it.

"Ye'll be a fun one, Grant."

And then he was gone, pushing away from the table, lumbering toward the door, and leaving me much relieved not to have been kissed by his foul mouth.

CHAPTER NINETEEN

Emma

"You must let me inside." The guards on either side of the corridor shifted their gazes away awkwardly as I pounded frantically outside of Ewan's door. "I have to speak with him," I said to them.

One took pity on me and responded, "My lady, he is not well. Ye canna speak to him."

"You don't understand. I *have* to speak with him."

The guard looked irritated, but held it in well, other than the slight twitch he'd developed in his eye and the corner of his lip. "My lady—"

The door to the chamber opened and Agatha peered into the hallway, her mouth turned down. "My lady," she murmured, her eyes raised as though surprised to see me there, or maybe surprised the guards had not allowed me entrance.

187

"Ye can come inside to attend him." She opened the door wider and allowed me to enter.

"Thank you," I murmured, looking down at the ground so as not to affront the guard. He'd done a good job of protecting me and if he was half as insistent while watching my door as he'd been with me not seeing Ewan, I was grateful.

The room was lit by candles, and smelled of blood and ointments. The healer stood beside Ewan packing a green paste into one of his many wounds. He was stripped to the waist, a coverlet pulled to his hips. More than half his wounds had been sewn and dressed. He looked like a crudely put together doll, with so many black strings crisscrossing to hold his flesh together.

His eyes were closed, and his breathing looked slightly less ragged than it had in the great hall. His pallor had not improved, however, and his lips were still grayish.

"Will he live?" I asked, my stomach churning at the pain he must be enduring.

The healer didn't respond, simply continued to apply the salve.

I glanced at Agatha, panic welling in my chest. "Well?"

"We canna be certain, my lady. He's been badly beaten. In truth, if we'd not found him within the hour we did, he'd have died. The man has ye to thank for it, for no one would have gone to search so soon if ye'd not insisted."

I waved away her admonitions. I found it odd that no one would have gone looking for the man in charge. Though, perhaps they were all confident in his abilities, and would have assumed he was doing what needed to be done. "Never mind that, I don't require thanks. Tell me how he's progressing."

Agatha pressed the back of her hand to his forehead. "Still has a fever. His body is fighting hard; it's not as high as it was before."

I stepped closer to the bed, took Ewan's free hand in mine and squeezed. His fingers fluttered in my grasp and he murmured something.

"What did he say?" I asked, a little anxious.

The healer shook her head. "Nonsense."

But I had a feeling he was trying to say something important, that the message he intended to get across was garbled by the wounds in his body.

"I think he's trying to tell me something," I insisted. I leaned over him, pushing my hair behind my ear and pressing it close to his lips. "Tell me, Ewan."

His breath puffed on my ear, and he issued an inaudible mumble.

"Ewan, tell me. You can do it, I believe in you. Logan is in trouble. I need you," I said.

"Logan," he whispered and that time I wasn't the only one to hear it.

The healer's hands stilled her movements, and Agatha gasped.

"Aye, Logan. He needs you," I said.

"Isabe... danger." His words puffed out between short pants. "She's..." He trailed off, swallowing hard.

I stroked a calming hand on his stubbled cheek, trying to reassure him as his breathing became labored. I was afraid the healer would push me away, tell me he needed to rest. But she ignored me, and I wondered if the woman had heard him say these things before. If she wanted me to hear them and alert the guards.

Ewan struggled a moment, grunting as he shifted uncomfortably. "Planning an... invas..."

"An invasion?" I asked, trying not to sound too freaked out as I imagined warriors climbing the walls and slicing down every man, woman and child in their path. I had no doubt that

Logan's vicious enemies would do it, too. They were heartless, seeing only a goal ahead and not caring how they reached it.

"Aye," Ewan choked, going into a coughing fit. Blood seeped from the side of his mouth and I reached out, Agatha stuffing a small linen into my palm.

I wiped at the blood, swallowing down my tears. "Shh... You don't have to say anything more now," I soothed. And he didn't. What he'd said was enough to get me moving and motivate the guards to do exactly as I said.

Ewan shook his head, gripped tight to my hand, the most strength I'd felt from him since coming into the room. He wasn't letting me go. His eyes popped open, searching until he found me. They were bloodshot, pain-filled.

"Did she do this to you?" I asked.

He nodded.

Fury, pure and powerful jolted through my blood. Isabella was even more vicious than I'd previously believed.

"We'll lock her away," I stated firmly.

Still he struggled, as though he wanted to say more.

"Water," I said, and Agatha reached for a pewter mug, handing it to me.

I held the cup to his lips and Ewan drank a small sip, aspirating some of it and coughing violently. More blood sprayed onto his lips. "Slowly, Ewan," I whispered.

He drank another few sips then laid his head back against the pillows, exhausted.

"The laird..." he murmured.

"Shh... We will get him."

Again, Ewan shook his head. "She said... she said they..."

My heart skipped a beat. There was more that I needed to know. More to Isabella's vicious attack than simply doing away with Logan's second in command.

"They'll kill him," he finally managed to say.

"Who? The king?" I asked, desperate now for an answer.

Ewan nodded again. Isabella had confessed this to him as she thought he lay dying. There was every possibility she spoke the truth, wanting to gloat about her plans to someone who could do nothing but listen. My gut told me that she'd relayed the truth to Ewan. Which meant…

"Oh my God." I staggered backward. My visions of Logan flooded my mind. I'd been right. They were true and he could be dead even now.

I wasn't the only one shocked. The healer's hands stilled and she glanced up at me, fear in her eyes. Agatha gasped and gripped tight to the side table as though she might fall.

"Rest now, Ewan. I will save the laird."

Three sets of eyes looked at me as though I'd grown two additional heads, but I nodded, shoulders squared. Determined.

"I won't let him die." Whirling, I marched toward the door and flung it open. To the guard there, I said, "Ewan has spoken. Lady Isabella was his attacker. She plans to let our enemies within the walls and did confess to him that the king has plans to kill Logan."

The guards' eyes hardened as they shifted their glances between them.

"Ewan has issued orders for the lady to be remanded to the dungeon. Double the forces on the walls and get a party together to ride to Falkland Palace to bring home our laird."

The guards nodded and three took their leave to go about the orders, and to send another guard up in case Isabella was found lurking about. The fourth remained behind to watch over Ewan's chamber.

I bowed my head in thanks, then turned back to the room. "All will be well. It's in the fates."

I waited at the door until another guard arrived, not that I'd be much help in subduing an attacker should they try to gain entry, but if it were Isabella, I'd knock her out.

191

The guard arrived quickly, taking his post beside the door and I couldn't help but ask, "Has she been taken?"

"Not yet, my lady."

I frowned, and rushed to my room to dress. Adrenaline and anger fueling my body's energy. I wanted to watch them lock her up. I wanted to see her behind bars. See her pockets emptied of any poison she might slip the guards. Isabella was not to be trusted a millimeter.

Leaving my chambers, I checked with the guards at Ewan's door once more. No word yet. I raced down the stairs toward the great hall, finding a great many of the servants and clan folk gathered, worry etching their faces.

"All will be well," I kept repeating, but my words offered little comfort. Their laird was gone and Ewan was badly injured.

Moments later we could all hear the bitch's screams from a far corridor. They'd gotten her. I couldn't help but hiss, "Yes!"

The sound of her anger made me smile. I rushed to the spot, pleased to see her trussed up like a pig. A guard walked in front of those who held her captive — perhaps to open the doors so those holding her didn't have to let go. Two guards dragged her, her back to where they were headed, but she had to have known it was over. Must have given the guards some fight, too, for them to have tied her up, but then again, maybe not. The tall guard to her left, I recalled, was the brother of one of the poor guards she'd gotten drunk and was subsequently punished for getting drunk.

Isabella's eyes landed on me, and she quieted, forcing all the guards to turn and see me standing there. Torchlight flickered on her face. Her lip curled cruelly as she watched me.

"He fucked me. Did ye know that?" she asked.

Stunned, I stopped walking. "Ewan?" I asked.

Slowly, she shook her head. "Nay, bitch, the laird."

Was it possible to feel like you'd been kicked in the stomach just from a few words? It took all the power I had not to double over from shock. No. She was lying. Logan would never betray me.

"Fucked me good and hard. Told me he was going to see the king about a contract for us. I may now be carrying his heir." She pursed her lips, giving me a pitying gaze. "Oh, dear. Did ye think he was going to gain the king's assistance for ye?" She shook her head and laughed. "Ye're even dumber than I thought."

At that moment the guards seemed to come to their senses and yanked her forward more. "Shut up, ye cow," the slighted guard hissed.

"'Tis all right, I've said enough." She pressed her lips together, as though she'd not say another word. Then she smiled again, unable to resist in her need to spread more vicious lies. "The contract will be drawn up. The marriage will be valid since we've already consummated it. And then he dies. Probably dead already. This is my castle now, and ye'll all be executed for treating your mistress this way."

I finally found my feet and walked forward, keeping in time with the guards. This time, I smiled. "Your lies will get you nowhere, Isabella. Well, except to the dungeon and then on a ship back north."

"Ye'd do best to kill me, whore. For I will not stop until ye're dead," she ground out.

"That can be arranged," I mused, feigning indifference. The woman had the ability to make me see red, and imagine how I could implement each of the wicked torture instruments I'd seen in Logan's dungeon.

"Ask him, when ye see him. Ask if his cock was not covered in my virgin's blood. Let him tell ye the truth. He'll not lie to ye."

They pushed through the door to the dungeon, walking down the thin windy stair. I followed them in the dank, decrepit place. Holding my breath, and then mouth breathing, trying not to smell. They opened the cell door and thrust her in, without removing the ties that bound her. Good. She deserved it.

As they closed the cell and locked it, I leaned close to the bars and said, "You lose."

Then I reached through the iron bars and wrenched Logan's ring from her finger.

*T*hough daylight was waning, the men of Logan's clan wasted no time in preparing to travel to Falkland. We were on horseback within the hour, and rode through the night. Not used to riding, my legs and ass ached, burned, and I was sure that the skin between my thighs had been rubbed raw. I nodded off, nearly falling off my horse a dozen times, but somehow found the strength to remain awake.

And every so often I was haunted by Isabella's words. Were they true? She seemed so confident Logan would confess to me that he'd slept with her... It was enough to shake me, but I kept my nerves in check. She'd probably just said it to rile me up, knowing her words would scratch away incessantly in my mind. A slow kind of torture. Besides, I trusted Logan implicitly. He'd never do anything to hurt me.

When dawn broke over the horizon, we rested the horses for no more than two hours — and I slept like the dead during that time. Then we rode again, arriving that night at the edge of the forest, Falkland Palace just ahead.

After seeing Isabella locked into a cell, I'd taken the dagger to the secret stair, lit a torch and walked all the way down, fearful of demons and ghosts ready to take my life. Then I'd followed the runes on the doors until I reached the one with the design just like the one on my hip — a half moon.

My hands shook so bad it took me four times before I was able to push the key into the lock. But it clicked, easily opening and I jumped back, expecting bones or something nefarious to leap out at me, but all I saw was a black, ornately carved box, sitting on top of a velvet covered table, cobwebs and dust covering it.

I sheathed the key, snatched the box and ran like hell up the hundred stairs, so much so that my legs gave out when I reached the top. They still burned deep in the tissue from all the activity.

The box was now in a satchel tied to my horse, and anytime anyone got near me, I became frantic with panic. No one could have the box.

When we reached the castle, it was in an uproar. Men shouted, ran back and forth. Horses loitered unattended and there was shit everywhere — tipped over barrels, dumped supplies. Like people where just dropping their crap and leaving it there. Utter chaos.

"What's happening?" I asked.

Logan's men shrugged. Finally a man in livery approached. "The king is dead, long live the queen."

"The queen?" I asked, searching my memory for any bit of history I could recall. Oh my God! The baby! Mary, Queen of Scots...

Holy shit, was this for real?

I swallowed hard and glanced toward my guards who all looked suddenly stricken.

"We've come for our laird, the Guardian of Scotland."

The man shook his head, looking dastardly. "Not seen him nigh on a sennight."

He was lying. But he ran away before we could question him further.

I glanced around. How in the hell would we be able to find Logan in this utter mess? There was no one to show us the way, either. On the other hand, with the place being in chaos, we'd likely get in and out unseen.

An older woman standing by the stables caught my attention and when our gazes connected, she nodded her head at me. I stared back at her, was she looking at me? She nodded again and gave a little wave of her hand, but looked about her frantically as though she hoped no one had seen her signal to me.

I climbed off my horse, securing the satchel containing the box onto my back.

"What are ye doing, my lady? Ye must remain on your mount. 'Tis not safe," Logan's guard called to me.

I came around the side of Gregor's horse and motioned for him to come down.

"This place is in an uproar, no one will notice if I slip away. There is an older woman by the stables motioning to me. I think she might know where Laird Grant is. You all find out what happened to the men who traveled with him."

He shook his head vigorously. "Nay, I canna let ye go alone. 'Tis not safe. I'll come with ye, and have the men search for our warriors."

I shook my head. "Wait for me here."

He hesitated, then slipped a dagger up my sleeve. With a final, long stare, he nodded. "Dinna engage with anyone, but in case ye need it."

I squeezed his hand. "Thank you. Be ready to depart."

I don't know why I was so confident. Maybe it was the visions, or just plain stupidity, but my blood rushed with adrenaline and excitement. We were in the right place. I knew it deep in my soul, just as I knew I could break Logan free of whatever bound him here.

I rushed to the stables and the woman grabbed hold of my arm, her long bony fingers biting hard through the fabric of my cloak and gown.

"He is dying," she said.

I nodded, knowing this. Accepting it. And eager to reverse it.

Her eyes locked with mine. "Ye must take him away from here."

I nodded again. She pushed a scroll into my hands. "Take this. Afore the king died, I encouraged him to sign it. 'Tis Laird Grant's title and lands. He is to be a free man, but none of the guards have let him go. Revenge, I think."

My stomach did a little flip and I shoved the scroll into the satchel. "Take me to him."

CHAPTER TWENTY

Logan

"Here he is, lass."

The words barely registered in my mind. Sounded sort of like the old crone. But the candle in my cell had long since burned out.

There was a scratch, a hiss and spark and then light glowed eerie.

Was I having another vision?

"Logan!" Emma's voice sounded so real, loud. At any moment I expected fog to fill the room and her to walk through it. But instead, the candle light came closer.

Should I answer her, so she could find her way to me? Tell her to come closer? To let me see her face?

I opened my mouth, but my tongue was swollen once more, likely split and cracked from dehydration and the latest beating.

All of my skin appeared to be in tact so at least I'd been spared the brutal warden's twenty-two cuts.

Even still, speaking was too painful.

I groaned, my eyes closing. I was having a vision, I was almost certain and keeping my eyes open to disappointment was simply too much.

"Oh, darling, I'm here. I won't leave you. Stay with me," Emma said.

Soft hands fluttered over me. A woman's hands. I kept my eyes closed, waiting for the hallucination to leave me. I couldn't bear it. Couldn't bear to see her and tell her we'd never be together again.

I was dying.

Only reprieved from execution when my torturer was called away. But he would return. He'd promised to. And then he'd resume what he'd started, and hopefully, I'd lose consciousness before he really gutted me.

Sawing sounds came from my wrist. Good God, the man had chosen to dismember me first. Not woman's hands at all, but my mind's way of coping with the pain of my new reality. I felt the pressure, waiting for the blade to begin its cut into my flesh.

But the waiting was too much.

I did open my eyes then, turning to the side to witness what he was doing. To meet his eyes with defiance as he attempted to unman me. I wasn't going down like that.

But it wasn't the man! *Emma*, I shouted in my mind what I couldn't say aloud as only a grunt passed my lips.

"Shh," she crooned as she cut away at the leather straps, freeing my hands.

It was working. That could mean only one thing—she was actually *here*. How had she made that happen?

A rush of painful tingles centered in my palms and fingers once the leather snapped open. So tight had the bindings been, it was an amazing rush of relief to feel them gone, enough so that I was able to ignore that sudden rush of agony.

I flexed my fingers, wincing in pain at the few that had been broken.

"We'll get ye out of here and then I can work to bind your wounds, my laird." The old crone spoke that time. I flicked my gaze to find her sawing at the bindings near my ankles. The women whispered in hushed, panicked, tones.

"I dinna… want it," I growled at the old woman.

They stilled their motions and she flicked her gaze up at me. "Ye dinna want to be free?" she asked.

Emma, too, looked completely stricken.

"I dinna want to be king," I somehow managed to say, though it sounded foreign to my ears.

"As ye wish," the old woman said, then continued to help Emma with the bindings, and I didn't resist, trusting that even if the old woman didn't want to hear my desires, Emma would.

The same familiar and painful tingle rushed up and down the arches of my feet when she finally got them free.

"We must hurry," the old lady said. "Most of the king's prisoners will be set free, but not ye, my laird. The executioner has his eye on ye for a treat. Come, lass, we must help him up."

Gentle hands on either side of my shoulders tried to lift me, but though I'd been beaten and starved for nearly two weeks, I was still a large man.

The women grunted with exertion, and I did, too, intent on sitting up on my own. I tried to balance on my elbows, to use my core muscles to sit up, but nothing seemed to be working right. I was as weak as a bairn. Even a lamb could walk within minutes of being born, and I couldn't even sit up.

The women pulled and pushed at me gently, never failing in their insistence that the deed would be done, though I wanted to order them gone. To forget about me. At last, I was sitting.

Emma gasped at the sight of my back. I didn't even want to know what it looked like. For they'd whipped me severely, and no one had come to tend those wounds, which were likely infected.

"His shirt, lass. Stop gawking or we'll never get it done."

The women tossed a shirt over my head and put my arms through it. They swept the fabric softly over my back, and still I hissed.

Emma gasped. "Logan! I'm so sorry..."

I grunted, tried to smile, but I was afraid it came out more like a grimace.

Not bothering with a plaid, they pulled my legs over the side of the table and stuffed my feet into braies, hose, and boots.

"Ye must gather your strength, my laird. Ye must stand," the older woman said.

"Wait, hold onto my shoulders." Emma took my arm and flung it across her back and shoulders and helped as I worked hard to hoist myself onto my feet.

Perhaps with a bit too much effort as I lurched forward, my body threatening to crush both women beneath me—my cock swaying in the breeze and my arse up in the air.

"Steady now," the older woman said, sounding as though she spoke to a mule or some other wild animal.

I didn't want to put all my weight on Emma. Didn't want to seem so helpless. But I was. And I did.

I leaned on her heavily as the old bat stuffed my twig and berries into the braies and tied the garment closed. Embarrassment had long since left me. They slipped a hooded cloak over me and then the old lady took the lead, ushering us forward.

"With all the chaos, 'twill nay be too difficult for ye to escape unseen by Garbhan, my laird."

"Garbhan?" Emma asked.

"His torturer. The man has it set in his mind to…keep Logan for some time."

I shuddered, having a good idea of what Garbhan had in mind. None of which would be pleasant whatsoever. "What chaos?" I asked, my mind still buzzing. It took every ounce of strength I had not to collapse. Every muscle screamed out in agony. My skin felt flayed.

Even though they'd rescued me, I'd still be lucky to make it out alive.

"The king is dead," Emma whispered. "Long live the queen."

My mind froze and I couldn't take another step forward.

James was dead?

The tormenter of my life no longer existed in this world? And I'd not been the one to run him through. Disappointment was an understatement. I was devastated.

I collapsed to my knees, my hand sliding down Emma's arm. Drained of energy and now of my soul, I'd never be able to face him. Never be able to seek vengeance on the man who'd tortured me for so long. The man who wanted me dead. Garbhan be damned, James was my true enemy.

Why the hell did he have to go and die? *I* deserved to kill him. It was my right to put him in his grave. *I* deserved to take back my life. My shoulders slumped, hands down on the ground. There would be no closure for me in this. How could I move on after being treated like an animal when I couldn't face the man who put me there?

Emma dropped beside me, her soothing hands on my face and she turned me to look at her. Her fiery hair framed her face in wild disarray. Porcelain skin was pale, lips a perfect red bow. Her green eyes flashed knowing as she pressed her palm to my cheek. I turned my lips into her hand, kissing the tender flesh there, and breathing in her lemon scent. She understood how I felt. She didn't pity me for it, she just offered herself as comfort.

My eyes burned with long held in tears, and even now I refused to let them leak. To do so would be showing how weak I felt, and I refused to let that be seen. Not even when I was broken.

I leaned toward her, pressed my face to her breast and breathed in her sense, the familiar sense of calm I felt whenever she was near coming over me. I wrapped my arms around her middle to hold her tight, every possibility I would never let go.

"What's this?" I asked, feeling the hard box within the satchel at her back.

She looked at me, her eyes wide, and she didn't speak.

Instantly, I knew what it was. "We must burn it."

Her throat bobbed and she gave a single nod of agreement.

With the evidence of who I was burned, there would be only one other thing I required. "I...need...to..." My throat was so tight, I could barely make the sound come out. "See him." I managed.

Emma shook her head. "You can't, Logan. There's no time. We have to get you out of here before they kill you."

I gazed at Emma, her brow crinkled with fear and worry, and I hated that I was the reason for her distress, but in this I would not back down. "Let them. I will see... his body."

Speaking made my throat ache, and I licked my cracked lips.

Emma chewed her lip, making me regret the growl of cruel words. She glanced up at the old woman who handed me a flask.

I took a long draught of whisky, feeling it burn a painful, then numbing path all the way to my stomach.

"Ye canna, lad. There are guards surrounding the place. They'll capture ye before ye get close."

"Let them," I said on a breath, then took another long pull from the flask.

I wasn't going to back down.

The old crone growled and I thought for a moment to feel a wallop on the back of my head like my nurse had done when I was a child.

"What is your name?" I asked her.

"Hilde."

I grunted and took another sip of whisky.

"Will ye be satisfied with a hole in the wall?" she asked.

I nodded, knowing anything more than that would mean my death and possibly Emma's and the old woman who was determined to help me.

The two women whispered as I crawled to the wall and worked to stand, using the stones to balance me. Emma rushed over and put my arm around her shoulder again. Then they scurried me along, stopping anytime they heard a noise. The corridors in the king's dungeon were short and windy, and we quickly came to a damp stairwell lit with a single torch and covered in rats.

"The warden sees fit to keep the critters around for the benefit of the residents," Hilde said with a short, bitter laugh.

Having worried they'd climb the table to nibble my toes, and fairly certain one or two had, I was not amused. Emma stifled a sound I knew was close to a scream as she meandered the steps with me adding to her weight. When we reached the top, Hilde held her hand up, stilling us both.

"All right, now ye go," Hilde said and scurried round the corner to the left.

Emma and I followed her into a darker corridor, only the light from the top of the dungeon stairs guiding our way. Moments later we were pitched into dark, as she grabbed hold of my hand and led us through a door and up a narrow, equally dark, stairwell. Servant's stairs most likely.

"Step lightly, now. We'll come to the top and then I'll take ye to a place to look in."

At the top of the stairs, she opened a door and our eyes quickly adjusted to the new light of a well-lit corridor. A dark green, woven carpet lined the corridor, silencing our footfalls.

Voices called to and fro, and Hilde stopped moving, issuing us a, "Shh..."

I took the reprieve to catch my breath. My heart pounded, blood rushed and breath was labored. So many stairs and so little strength to surmount them. I felt weak, cowardly. This wasn't me. I loathed my brother all the more for bringing me so low.

"Now," Hilde said, yanking us forward across the hall. "Against the wall. Slide down five feet and then slip into the alcove. Ye can see from there."

I did as she instructed with Emma by my side. Inside the alcove, I felt along the darkened wall until I found a little nob, and I pulled it back. Six inches into the wall was a hole cut away and light filtered through. Closing one of my puffy eyes, I could barely see into the room. But seconds later as my vision adjusted, I could see very clearly. The king's prone body on a bed. His hands folded over his chest as he lay in state. His best robes of red and gold, his jewels and crown adorning him. Eyes closed, James looked more peaceful than I'd ever seen him before in my life.

Priests walked back and forth along the length of him, swinging their silver balls of incense and murmuring prayers.

He was dead. The king, my brother, dead. And I was rightfully king.

But I didn't want it. Wouldn't take it. I'd rather sink quietly back to my keep and live my life in peace with Emma.

I was reminded then who awaited me at the castle — Isabella — and what she'd done to me before I left.

I had to tell Emma the truth, it was imperative she know. Especially now that I'd recalled all of what happened during our interlude. The wretched MacDonald woman.

I turned to Emma then, wanted her to have the choice of leaving me here if she felt the need to, though nothing had occurred, other than a woman trying to play me false.

I faced her in the dark, sensing where she was. "Emma..."

"Oh, Logan, I'm so glad you're alive," she whispered, kissing me lightly on the lips.

"I have to tell ye something."

"It can wait," she replied.

"Nay, it canna. 'Tis about Isabella."

In the darkened of the alcove, I felt rather than saw her face falter, the energy somehow leaving her.

"She told me," Emma murmured.

"All of it?"

"Yes."

My stomach dropped. Even knowing all of Isabella's lies she'd still come after me.

"Ye must listen..."

"Shh, not now, Logan. Let's get out of here first."

I shook my head and reached for her shoulders, pulling her toward me. "'Tis all lies, love. She tried. She drugged me. But I remember everything. I remember her shoving me to the floor, of her trying to..." I short laugh escaped me. "'Twas the first time I'd not gotten hard for a willing wench. And I never thought I'd be grateful for such a thing. I could never betray ye, lass. Even poisoned, my body responds only to ye."

"Logan," Emma said, pressing her forehead to the crook of my neck, her arms sliding around me. "I never believed her. And even if it had been true, I wouldn't have left you here to die."

"We must go," Hilde hissed from outside the alcove.

Renewed strength filled me, and I pressed a little less weight on Emma as we traced our steps back to the servants' stair and down to the courtyard. Hilde summoned my men closer. Those who'd accompanied me had been found in the dungeon, and though they looked a little worse for wear, none of them were in bad shape.

All held horrified expressions when they saw me. I feared what I might see in the reflection of the loch.

"He canna make the journey to Gealach like that," Gregor said. I was surprised but pleased to see him. He must have accompanied Emma. I tried to argue that I'd make it, but all of them naysaid me.

"We must find a shelter where he'll be safe and can be healed," Gregor said to Emma.

I couldn't have been more proud that they looked on her with such respect. She'd risked her life to come after me, and she'd found me. To them, she was a goddess, just as she'd always been to me.

"I know a place," Hilde said. "'Tis my cottage. Deep in the wood, no one will look there for him."

The men looked skeptical, turning to myself and Emma once more.

"Let us go there," I said.

Within a quarter hour, we were half a mile from Falkland and on our way to freedom.

CHAPTER TWENTY-ONE

Logan

Four weeks later

*W*e arrived back at the castle in mid-afternoon.

As we rode past the clan who'd gathered in droves from the gate to the castle stairs, they bowed, they called out greetings and prayers. Most of them looking to Emma as their savior.

I, too, stared at her. "Ye saved us, love."

She blushed and smiled. "No, Logan. We did it together."

I smiled, giving in to her, though I knew that without her, I wouldn't be where I was. Likely, I'd be in the hands of that fucking lunatic beneath Falkland Palace, but I needn't disappoint her with that knowledge.

We were greeted not only by the swift shouts and elated calls of the clan, but by Ewan himself. He stood at the top of the entrance stairs, leaning against the large wooden doors to the keep. A huge grin split his face. I was relieved to see him standing there, to know that he'd not died at Isabella's hands. For such a thing to happen would have been my own fault.

"Glad we are to have ye back, my laird. As well ye, my lady," he called.

"Glad we are to finally have returned," I said.

Ewan's grin faltered. "Ye have a visitor, my laird."

Not the words I wanted to hear.

I dismounted, then came around to Emma's side and held up my hands, loving the warmth and weight of her in my arms. I set her on the ground, but couldn't let her go. With my arm around her waist we approached the stairs and Ewan.

"Who awaits us?" I asked.

Ewan had lost his smile completely now, his face grim. "MacDonald. He's come to collect his niece."

I gave a curt nod. "Emma, darling—"

"No. I'm coming," she said, cutting me off before I could even ask her to let me handle it on my own.

"All right. But if there be bloodshed, promise me, ye'll await me in our chamber."

Emma stared hard into my eyes, and I could guess at any number of things she was saying in her mind. I grinned, and she rolled her eyes, but nodded anyway.

"Where is he?" I asked Ewan.

"Under guard in the great hall."

I did not waste time in greeting my mortal enemy. I wanted him out of my castle and far from here within the hour.

MacDonald stood center, blustering in the great hall, murder his eyes. He looked thinner than the last time I'd seen him, and he was in need of a good scrubbing. It felt good to see the man brought down a few notches.

I walked with Emma to stand by the chairs my men had set out for us both, the one I sat in to hear the requests and complaints of my people. We didn't sit down.

"Ye've been beaten," I said. "Sadly, the king has gone, and in his place a daughter rules."

"A regent rules for her," MacDonald spat.

"Aye. A protestant regent, the next in line for the throne and no friend of yours. Pity really, that all your well laid plans should be burned to ash." I held tight to Emma's hip. She was the only reason I didn't challenge this man to a duel right then and there.

MacDonald spit on the floor. A staunch Catholic, he was bound to have issues with a Protestant ruler. And he'd not be the only one.

"I am still Guardian of Scotland," I said. This time I did let go of Emma. Stalking forward, I stopped within a foot of my enemy. "And I see ye as a threat to the country."

Though the hatred still remained in his eyes, they ebbed with something new. Fear.

"Guards!" I called. "Take him to the dungeon where he can be reunited with his niece."

"Ye canna do this. My men await me! If I'm not back within the hour, they'll attack!"

Ewan cleared his throat. "Pardon, my laird, but MacDonald's men also await him in the dungeon."

I smiled cruelly at the vicious old dog. "Then ye may debrief with them when ye arrive."

"Bastard!" he sneered. If he'd had a dagger, the man would have tried to stab me to death, of that I was certain.

I leaned in closer and spoke in low tones. "On the contrary, I think ye know exactly who I am."

MacDonald's eyes widened. "'Tis true, then!"

I didn't respond, but turned my back on him, returning to Emma and leading her out of the great hall.

"Dinna turn your back on me, Grant! Dinna dare!"

I didn't stop, but kept going. The man would likely always be a thorn in the underside of my foot, but never again would he have the backing of our sovereign.

Behind me I heard the distinct whisper of metal on leather. I nudged Emma forward and whipped around in time to see that MacDonald had pulled a hidden blade from within his belt. My men all moved to pounce, but a flick of my wrist and they backed off. I drew a blade from my sleeve.

"Ye want to fight then, MacDonald? I'll even let it be a fair fight. Dagger against dagger. Ye'll never walk out of my hall again. I gave ye a chance." I shrugged. "Now, ye've drawn on me, and I've no choice but to end your miserable life."

Behind me, I heard Emma squeak, reminding me of my vow of peace.

"Love, if ye would, wait for me upstairs," I said.

I don't know if she left or not, but I couldn't concentrate on that. I had to dispatch of this giant rat once and for all, peace be damned.

"Your call," I taunted. "I but await ye."

MacDonald growled, his cheeks growing ruddy as he circled me, arms up in defensive mode, his blade glinting in the candlelight.

He lunged toward me, slashing viciously with his blade. I jumped out of the way at the last second, but his blade did catch my shirt, tearing it at the shoulder, but missing my flesh all together. For a man easily a decade older than I, he was quick. But not quick enough. He didn't scare me. Only made the fight all the more challenging.

I retaliated with my elbow to his brow, and my dagger slicing along his ribs. I didn't stab him, just a slice. I changed my mind. I didn't intend to kill him, nor to mortally wound him. Only to punish him for challenging me. Give him a minor fraction of a taste of what I'd had to endure. Drawing attention to myself now would ruin all the plans I had—plans for peace and days on end in bed with Emma.

I bounded back, ready for his next move. The man growled and lunged again, ducking at the last minute to slice at my shins, but I kicked his hand away, his dagger clattering across the floor. A flash of fear showed in his eyes, as he stared up at me. But I slowly backed away, allowing him a chance to reacquire his weapon.

MacDonald might have been fast, but did he really think with as many attacks as we had on our castle that I wouldn't be able to easily deflect his moves? I trained my men to protect the king. I trained men to fight half a dozen warriors at once. Fighting against one Highlander was like sending a squire into a room full of hussies and not expecting him to come out a man. Ridiculous.

My enemy's face grew red with anger and he bared his teeth at me as he jumped to his feet, dagger retrieved. We made two more circles, but I refused to make the first move. This was his fight.

MacDonald lunged forward again, but this time, he twirled in the opposite direction at the last minute, hoping to catch me off guard. He nearly did, but I was fast, too. I turned with him, slicing his other side.

That only made the old dog angrier and instead of backing away, he went at me again, punching with his free hand, and trying to stab at my heart with his weapon.

Enough was enough. I bellowed and head-butted MacDonald square in the center of his forehead. I hit him hard, seeing the room spin for a second as I braced myself not to fall. The blow took MacDonald completely by surprise and he stumbled backward, dropping his knife, and grabbing at his head, the skin split above his brow.

He clutched at his head and fell to his arse, a loud oomph issuing from his wretched mouth.

I walked over to him, and pressed my foot to his chest, pushing him backward. Still stunned, he fell back, and I kept my foot on his chest.

"Dinna challenge me, MacDonald. I *always* win." I glanced up at my men who looked on without a trace of thought on their faces. "Send this heathen and his wayward niece home. No need for niceties. They can ride chained in the brig of the galley. Drop them at one of the beaches of Pentland Firth and let them find their own way home."

"Ye son of a bitch! Ye'll pay for this!"

"Likely, ye'll try to attack me again, and likely ye'll lose. Though, next time I will nay show ye mercy. Next time I will slice ye in two and feed ye to the cats in the hills."

I nodded to my men who came forward and trussed MacDonald up. The bastard was lucky I'd decided to turn a new leaf, as Emma put it. He screamed insults and threats as they dragged him away. But all I could do was laugh. The man was madder than a cornered wildcat. I was actually looking forward to his revenge—and taking his life.

When I turned, I thankfully found that Emma had listened to me. I rushed up the stairs, rounding them two at a time. I found her waiting inside, staring out the window. As soon as she heard me, she whirled and ran toward me, launching herself in my arms. Neither of us spoke, but stood there silent, holding each other tight for several heart-pounding moments.

Then I released her, and poured us each a glass of wine.

"To us, and our new beginning," I said.

Emma raised her glass. "To us, and a destiny fulfilled."

"Nay, just beginning." I winked and we clinked out glasses, sipping the wine.

Emma stepped forward and wiped something from my forehead. "We could both use a bath."

Without hesitation, I stalked to the door, opening it and ordering a bath to be brought in, not bothering at all to make a show of modesty. I wanted to soak in the warm water with Emma. We'd had little privacy at Hilde's cottage, and we'd not made love in the flesh in nearly two months.

My body was on fire for her. Holding the roundness of her hip in my palm was enough to get my blood stirring, cock hard. We stood before the hearth watching as servants rushed in and out with the tub and water. I was ready to disband with the washing and send them all away in favor of stripping Emma bare and worshiping her where we stood.

"Want me to wash you?" she asked, staring up at me.

I shook my head and she frowned.

I grinned. "I'm going to wash ye."

Her frown deepened. "You're the one who's in need of a tender touch."

I grinned even wider and leaned down so the servants wouldn't hear. "There's going to be a lot of touching, love."

Her face colored, rosy on her cheeks, and a fair blush on her neck.

"Oh…" she sighed, her eyes suddenly blazing fire.

"All right, enough," I boomed to the servants. "Out with ye. I can finish the rest."

They looked up, some surprised and some with knowing smiles. They finished up quickly and hurried out. I left Emma's side to shut the door in the protesting faces of both Hilde and Agatha. Both proclaiming their needs to tend to Emma, in an attempt to get me away from her. I knew what they were saying—in truth they did not believe she was a woman I should trifle with, and they were right.

I was through playing games. I wanted her for my own, forever.

"Time for your bath, my lady," I said, striding toward her.

CHAPTER TWENTY-TWO

Logan

*E*mma's sensual mouth curled in a smile. "I thought it would never be ready," she said.

I laughed, and when I reached her, turned her around so I could uncoil her hair and run my fingers through it. So soft. The scent of lavender drifted to my nostrils. I leaned close to breathe her in.

"Ye're the only reason I made it through that hell hole." I slid my hands over the curve of her shoulders, massaging the tension that had taken up residence. "The thought of ye, the memories, plans for the future. If not for ye, I might have given up."

She shook her head, her hair swaying, giving me brief glimpses of her silky neck. I leaned down and kissed the crook between her neck and shoulder. Emma sighed with pleasure and tilted her head to the side to give me better access to her flesh.

"You're more resilient than you know, Logan," she said. "Though you think you might have perished, I know you better than that. You're strong and you're loyal to your people. You wouldn't have allowed yourself to simply...die."

I scraped my teeth over to her shoulder and sucked at her flesh. She shuddered, reached up and slid her hand around the back of my neck.

"I dinna know, lass. There were times I think I might have."

"I'm glad you didn't."

"Me, too." I chuckled and turned her to face me. "I could never have left you."

Emma slid her hands up over my chest, sending frissons of deep yearning to rush through my veins. She wrapped her arms around my neck and leaned up on tiptoe. "I hope you never do again."

She closed the distance, kissing my lips tenderly. But all tenderness lasted a mere few seconds as I swept my tongue inside her mouth to taste her. That simple move caused a surge of hunger to discharge through us both. We clung tight to one another, mouths hungrily sliding over and again.

As we kissed, we tugged at the clothing blocking us from touching skin to skin. Her gown, chemise, my shirt and plaid, both our boots and hose, until we stood naked and flush together. The heat of our bodies singed as we rubbed against one another, our mouths still connected. A tantalizing torment. Her breasts crushed to my chest, hardened nipples scraping over my skin, and the warm, damp netherlips teasing my thickened cock.

I groaned, hands cupping her breasts, thumbs sliding over her cherry-ripe nipples. My mouth watered, like her body was the essence of life and I a dying man. I dipped down to taste her reddened pebble, flicking my tongue over it, circling it, then drawing it gently into my mouth. Emma cried out, arching her back, her hands threading in my hair. Her response to me was always so raw, powerful and filled with passion, sparking a parallel response in myself.

"I've wanted this," she panted, "for so long. It was torture not having you."

"Och, lass, ye have no idea." I feasted on one breast and then another. Slid my fingers along the inside of her thigh until I reached the dewy sweetness of her cunny. I groaned. My blood pumped, fueling me for an eternity with my desire for her.

I lifted her into the air, one arm beneath her knees and the other around her back. "Time for your bath, my lady, else I take ye right here on the chamber floor."

"You know, I can never have a bath without my body burning for you," she confessed.

"The sound of water makes my cock hard, for every trickle reminds me of water dripping on your silken, luscious body."

I practically ran to the tub, stepped inside and sank down with Emma facing away from me and settled between my thighs. Her buttocks pressed temptingly to my cock. I shifted back a little, but she only followed me.

I blew out a long breath, trying to regain some control. I wanted this to last. Didn't want to have it end so soon. If my cock had a mind of its own, I'd have slid inside her already.

With an arm tucked around her waist, I grabbed hold of the bar of soap and dipped it into the water. I slid the slick bar over Emma's shoulders, down between her breasts to her belly. She sighed, a slight shudder going through her, and she leaned her head back onto my shoulder, her eyes closing.

"I could get used to this," she murmured.

"Then we'll have to make it a regular activity."

"Oh, yes, please."

I smoothed the bar over her breasts, watching the suds bubble on her creamy skin and nipples. I set the bar down, content to run my hands over her slickened skin. To see how many bubbles I could create and pop.

Emma moaned, arching her back, her buttocks pressing harder to my groin. I gritted my teeth, turgid shaft pulsing with need.

I slid my fingers over her neck and shoulders. Pushing her forward, I stroked my soapy hands over her back, thumbs kneading the length of her spine. The ends of her hair were wet and tickled my hands and forearms.

Every inch of her felt exquisite, and she was all mine. I caressed my way to the base of her spine, over her hips to her smooth, flattened belly, then trailed my fingers down her thighs. Her legs fell open to the sides, and I couldn't help but take her up on her invitation. I cupped her heat, stroking my thumb over her clit and teasing the folds of her sex.

Emma gasped, writhing in my arms.

"I missed touching ye," I whispered in her ear. "The heat of ye, so slick and smooth."

I slid a finger inside her, feeling the muscles of her heat clenching me tight, then letting me go, then clenching again. I wanted to feel her do that on my cock.

"Turn around," I gently commanded.

Emma grabbed hold of the tub and lifted herself up, her beautiful, heart-shaped arse in my face. I playfully smacked her buttocks, and she shrieked and jumped around. Water sluiced down her belly, to the two bare lips of her sex, centering at the top and dripping in a line down the crack where her netherlips touched.

"Do ye know how beautiful ye are?" I asked, gaze flicking up to her face, then back down to her sex. I leaned forward, licking the line of her cleft, and gathering the droplets of water on my tongue.

Emma gasped, her knees buckling. I grabbed her hips, steadying her. But one lick wasn't enough. It never was with her. With the pads of my thumbs, I parted her folds, and gazed at the wondrous pink petals, the little nob that made her hiss when I touched it. I flicked my tongue over the knotted flesh, listening for that quick indrawn breath and chuckling with satisfied pleasure when it passed her lips.

I slipped a finger slowly inside her as I scraped my teeth gently over her clit. Emma moaned, a guttural, primal sound that I answered with a groan of my own, sucking gently on that bundle of nerves as I tongued her folds. I held tight to her hip, balancing her as she trembled and quaked. Heated cream slicked my fingers as I plunged in and out. She draped herself over me, hands on my shoulders, breasts on my head, hair tickling the top of my back. I was relentless in my pursuit of her pleasure. I lapped at her delicious body, the slippery folds, that bundle of nerves, all the while fucking her with one finger, then two, then stretching her further with three.

She moaned, panted, mumbled incoherent words. Her nails dug deep into my flesh. Every time I felt her body tense, I pulled my fingers out, mouth away, blew hotly on her sex, but didn't touch her. Counted to twenty, then dipped back in, teasing her with small nudges of my tongue and only one finger, before diving back in completely, loving her with my whole mouth and multiple fingers deep inside her.

After forcing her to hold back her climax several times, I gave into her trembling, aching need and drove her over the edge. Head thrown back, beautiful body taught, she peaked. An erotic cry that thrummed along every nerve in my body like the swipe of her delicious tongue, poured from her lips. Her sex held my fingers tight as she spasmed around me. Emma's completion was glorious, wonderful and had me nearly climaxing just to behold it.

Grabbing hold of her hips, I tugged her down, her knees straddling my hips, my cock notching against her entrance. "I love ye," I said.

Emma kissed me hard, licking her juices from my lips and tongue, and thrusting her pelvis downward, my cock filling her. "I love you, too," she said.

She felt so good surrounding me. Tight, warm, wet. Like home. If I could, I'd stay buried inside her for the rest of my life. I held onto her hips, steadying her pace, but when I'd teased her before, she now returned the favor, ignoring the pace I set, she bounced on me rapidly. Water sloshed over the sides of the tub, but I didn't care. A casualty of our war on pleasure.

The muscles of her sheath clenched tight around me with every downward move, and I swore I was going to explode every time. She was doing that thing she'd been doing on my fingers. Tightening, releasing, tightening, releasing. Gritting my teeth, I squeezed my eyes shut and kissed the hell out of her at the same time I forced myself not to come.

When Emma sucked in a ragged gasp and her body stiffened as she hastened her pace, I knew we were at the end, and I no longer had to hold back. I growled, crying out with the force of my body shattering. My orgasm gripped me tight and held on strong as I pumped up into her, matching her frantic rhythm. At that same moment, Emma too cried out, her body jerking forcefully.

We stayed in the water until our skin prickled and pruned, and then we climbed out, drying each other before the hearth. As I knelt before Emma, looking up at her pink, love-ripened skin, I was overcome with my love for her.

"Will ye marry me?" I asked her.

A broad grin covered her lips. "Is this an official proposal?" she asked.

"Aye, lass. I know I've said it before. But now I would make it happen without waiting. I want ye to be my wife. I love ye."

"I love you, too."

"When I stared death in the face, all I could think about was not wanting to leave ye behind. When I think about the rest of my life, I canna imagine it without ye in it. Ye've shared my deepest, darkest secrets. Ye've seen me at my lowest, and ye've seen me at my highest. Hell, woman, ye traveled through the bounds of time and space. Emma, love, ye've changed my whole world. Ye've changed who I am, who I want to be. And all for the better. I'd not realized how lost I was until I met ye. How hopelessly broken I was. Ye made me whole again and I want to spend the rest of my life making ye happy."

"Oh my God, Logan!" Tears welled in her eyes and I leapt to my feet, gathering her in my arms. "I want to spend the rest of my life with you, too. You're my everything. You showed me how to love again, how to be strong. I can't live without you."

I swiped at the tears gathering on her cheeks and kissed her hard on the mouth. "As soon as we rise, we'll make it happen."

She beamed. "I wish it were morning already."

My heart pounded, booming within my chest. "How should we pass the time?" I wiggled my eyebrows and gave her a wicked grin.

Emma winked naughtily. "I know several ways." She turned and scurried toward the bed, jumping up onto it on all fours. Turning her head around toward me, she wiggled her arse. "Want to start here?"

Oh, Lord, did I ever.

EPILOGUE

Emma

With nervous excitement, I let Hilde and Agatha argue over who would braid my hair, and then which color ribbons they'd weave within it. Hilde wanted gold to reflect the highlights in my hair. Agatha wanted green to match my eyes. In the end, they chose both.

Another beautiful gown had been pulled from Logan's foster mother's chest—her wedding gown. It was elegant, gorgeous, and probably the prettiest dress I'd ever had. Made from ivory wool—like cashmere—seed pearls were clung to the neckline, wrists and hem by gilded thread. The bodice was fashioned from the clan's colors—green and red with thin stripes of dark blue. I was mesmerized, and so were my two mother hens.

Hilde had returned with us just the day before, to Gealach Castle, and the two older women had not stopped bickering since meeting. About everything. Me. Logan. Food. Drinks. Clothing. It was ridiculous, but beneath all their bluster, I could see the beginnings of a dear friendship.

Logan's body had healed, though I feared for his heart. I never doubted that he loved me. Never doubted for a second on that account, but since we'd rescued him from that dark dungeon, he'd scowled and brooded far more than he ever had before.

All of his broken bones, torn flesh and bruises, his weakened state, took weeks to heal, far longer than he wanted, but with both Hilde and I making him rest, he had no other choice. Well, that wasn't really true. If he'd wanted to get up and walk out, I doubted there was anything the two of us could have done to stop him.

Half his guards remained behind at the tiny cottage deep in the woods that belonged to Hilde. There she'd whipped up her potions, lotions and ointments and sewn Logan up. With Hilde's care and regular meals, Logan had mended. His body was riddled with new scars, but they were battle wounds he bore proudly, because he was still alive.

I was shocked to see that they bowed to me, not just Logan. They respected me. They trusted me. They looked up to me. Not something I'd ever expected. And it felt good. I'd wanted to be a part of them, hadn't realized how much. Now I belonged. I had a family.

I was elated at finding Ewan healthy and walking around. Watching Logan and Ewan side by side looked like a pair that had walked from one end of the earth to the other. Both a little beat up and pale, but showing the world their strength, their passion for life and for their people.

But the most change came when Logan chose not to kill MacDonald when he could have. He proved that he was still deadly when he fought the man. As much as I'd seen. I ran from the room, but couldn't keep completely away. I watched from one of the spy holes as Logan thwarted the asshole.

He'd not ended the man's life, choosing peace. It made me smile. Logan really was trying to change his life. He wanted us to live peacefully in this new reign. And so it began.

In our chamber when Logan knelt down on his knee and proposed, his heartfelt confession had torn into me, flayed me open.

How could I ever deny him? Or myself?

Then we'd made love. We'd feasted. We'd danced. We rejoiced.

"All done, now, lass," Agatha said.

"Aye, all done," Hilde piped in.

I rolled my eyes and stood from the bench.

"Thank you."

Someone knocked at the chamber door. Thank God, good timing. I could get away from these mother hens.

The older women rushed to the door and butted hips until one of them finally grasped the handle and opened it.

Ewan stood in the doorway looking in at the pair of them like they'd shape-shifted into monkeys.

"Ignore them," I said. "They've been jockeying for power since we got back."

All of them looked at me oddly, and I knew it was because they didn't understand what jockeying meant, but I suspected they got the gist of it as the two older women both flicked their gazes away, a little embarrassed.

I laughed and hugged them both tight, and whispered, "I've not had a mother in a long time. I'm more than happy to find I now have two."

Two pairs of arms wrapped around me, and I didn't dare squeak at the slight pull to my hair or the need for air.

"Are ye ready, lass?" Ewan asked.

"I've never been more ready in my life."

"I'd be honored to escort ye to the great hall then."

"Thank you." I took his offered arm and he led me from my chamber out into the corridor.

For a split second, I expected to see Isabella rushing toward me, dagger drawn, but there was only the flaming torches to greet us. That wench and her uncle were halfway to nowhere by now. Though, Logan was certain MacDonald would return, revenge on his mind. No doubt his niece would also seek vengeance. We'd be ready when they did. Together, we could conquer anything.

Down the stairs we went until we reached the crowded great hall that had been decorated with swaths of silky fabrics hanging over the walls and ceilings, vases of holly bushes, fir branches and herbs scented the air. The entire clan gathered for the ceremony. Our wedding.

A broad smile broke out on my face. This time around, my marriage would be real, meaningful and happy. There would be no fear, no power play, but pure love, pleasure and friendship.

Near the hearth stood the clan's priest and beside him, my dark, wickedly handsome laird. Soon to be my husband.

Today, I would bind myself completely to him and his world. Forever letting go of Emma Gordon and the twenty-first century Today, I'd become Lady Grant, mistress of Gealach, wife of the Guardian.

Ewan led me through the crowd and I smiled with pure joy at Logan, for it seemed every wish I'd dreamed of had come true.

He stood in full regalia, buffed leather boots, bared knees, red and green great kilt, flung over his shoulder and pinned with a large silver, Celtic knot brooch. His broad chest filled out a crisp new white linen shirt. Cleanly shaven face, and dark hair curling toward his collar. His eyes danced with merriment. Damn, but he was one sexy Scot.

My heart fluttered, skipped a beat and my mouth went dry. And then he smiled at me. The corner of his lip quirking up as his gaze roved over me appreciatively. Suddenly, I was hot all over, nipples hard, aching and my thighs clenching tight. I loved it when he looked at me like that. I felt wicked and delicious.

"I'm glad to have been here for your wedding," Ewan whispered beside me.

My gaze shot to his, and again I was struck by his eyes. Probably for the thousandth time. He was so like my brother Trey. An impossibility, but all the same, Ewan was like a brother to me.

"As opposed to being…?"

He winked. "I owe my life to ye, lass. The entire clan does."

I shook my head. "No, Ewan. No one owes me anything." I glanced up at Logan and smiled. "We are all destined to things, people, places. It is up to us if we choose to take our destinies seriously, or we let them slip away."

"Then I am grateful your destiny sent ye to us."

"As am I," Logan said as we'd reached the hearth. "Eternally grateful."

Ewan placed my hand on Logan's arm and then took a step away from us.

As one, Logan and I turned to face the priest.

It was just us two against the world. Together forever, in our own happily ever after.

"The End"

If you enjoyed **DARK SIDE OF THE LAIRD**, *please spread the word by leaving a review on the site where you purchased your copy, or a reader site such as Goodreads or Shelfari! I love to hear from readers too, so drop me a line at* <u>authorelizaknight@gmail.com</u> *OR*

visit me on Facebook:
https://www.facebook.com/elizaknightauthor. I'm also on
Twitter: @ElizaKnight. Sign up for my newsletter at
www.elizaknight.com do get updates on new releases and
contests. *Many thanks!*

Dark Side of the Laird

If you love Highlanders...

Check out Eliza Knight's Stolen Bride series!

The Highlander's Reward
The Highlander's Conquest
The Highlander's Lady
The Highlander's Warrior Bride
The Highlander's Triumph
The Highlander's Sin

Coming in early 2014 – The Highlander's Temptation

ABOUT THE AUTHOR

Eliza Knight is the multi-published, award-winning, Amazon best-selling author of sizzling historical romance and erotic romance. While not reading, writing or researching for her latest book, she chases after her three children. In her spare time (if there is such a thing...) she likes daydreaming, wine-tasting, traveling, hiking, staring at the stars, watching movies, shopping and visiting with family and friends. She lives atop a small mountain, and enjoys cold winter nights when she can curl up in front of a roaring fire with her own knight in shining armor. Visit Eliza at www.elizaknight.com or her historical blog History Undressed: www.historyundressed.com

Made in the USA
San Bernardino, CA
02 March 2014